The Flaxborough Novels

'Watson's Flaxborough begins to take on the solidity of Bennett's Five Towns, with murder, murky past and much acidic comment added.'

H. R. F. KEATING

Bump In The Night

'Chief Inspector Larch? My name is Purbright. Flaxborough CID. I expect the Chief Constable . . .'

'Of course, Mr Purbright.' Larch coldly appraised the man whose hand he shook. He was nearly as tall as himself, of slightly diffident manner and with a quick, apologetic smile. The fresh-complexioned face had a touch of foolish amiability about the mouth. Above grey eyes, steadily interested, it seemed, in what they saw, the high forehead was crowned with short but unruly hair of preposterous king-cup yellow.

'Yes, I'd heard you were being loaned to us in our distress.' Larch resumed his seat and waved Purbright to another. 'I only hope someone's told you what you're supposed to do. We' – he gestured largely with his hand – 'are baffled.'

The Flaxborough Novels

Whatever's Been Going On At Mumblesby?
Plaster Sinners
Blue Murder
One Man's Meat ★
The Naked Nuns ★
Broomsticks Over Flaxborough
The Flaxborough Crab
Charity Ends at Home
Lonelyheart 4122 ★
The Flaxborough Chronicle
containing: Hopjoy Was Here ★
           Bump In The Night ★
           Coffin Scarcely Used ★

★ *also available in Methuen Paperback*

COLIN WATSON

Bump In The Night

A Flaxborough Novel

Methuen

A Methuen Paperback

BUMP IN THE NIGHT
ISBN 0 413 55380 9

First published in Great Britain 1960
by Eyre & Spottiswoode Ltd
Copyright © 1960 by Colin Watson
This edition published 1984
and reprinted 1985
by Methuen London Ltd
11 New Fetter Lane, London EC4P 4EE

Printed and bound in Great Britain by
Richard Clay (The Chaucer Press) Ltd,
Bungay, Suffolk

1

THE FIRST OF THE CHALMSBURY BLOWINGS-UP TOOK place one warm, still night in early summer. It made the most godawful bang that had been heard in the town since a bewildered German pilot mistook the Parish Church for Lincoln Cathedral during a Baedecker raid and capped this undeserved compliment by dropping a bomb on the Food Office, a building of even less architectural merit.

Several people were awakened by the explosion, and many more by the frenzied barking of dogs that it provoked. A few disturbed sleepers got up and peered from their windows, but they saw no glow in the sky and heard no cries, no bells, no hurrying footsteps. Whatever had gone off, or up, did not seem to have left any situation worth their attention.

Only one man was sufficiently conscientious, or curious perhaps, to try and trace the source of the fearful noise that had sent him skipping out of bed, his brain flooding with confused memories of Home Guard manoeuvres, thunder storms, and an entertaining encounter his wife once had had with a boarding house geyser.

He was Councillor Oswald Pointer, wholesale wine merchant: a testy, bald-headed citizen of small stature but quite ferocious rectitude in matters affecting the security and convenience of the Chalmsbury ratepayer.

"This is Councillor Pointer speaking," emerged the thin, nasal announcement from the telephone that Sergeant Worple picked up at the police station in Fen Street. The words were edged with accusation, and the sergeant, soured by night duty, prepared to be as unhelpful as he dared. "Oh yes, sir," he responded stiffly.

"What was that?" demanded Pointer.

"What was . . . what, sir?" By the slightest of pauses in the middle of his counter-question Worple implied that he wasn't going to believe anything that the caller might tell him.

"Why, that infernal row, of course. That great bang. What was it?"

"You heard a . . . bang, sir?" The measured, butleresque query, heavy with respectful doubt, swung back at Pointer like a sandbag.

The councillor snorted angrily and shuffled his rapidly chilling bare feet on the carpet. "Look here, I'm telling you a damned great explosion woke me up a couple of minutes ago. I'm asking you if you know anything about it. I'm reporting it, if you like. Now do you understand?"

"Ah, you're making a report of an occurrence. Very well, sir. Will you hold the line a moment?" Worple put the telephone down on the desk with great deliberation, strolled to the far side of the room and returned slowly with a large book. "Your full name, now, if you please, sir."

"Pointer. Councillor Oswald Pointer. Oh, but surely. . . ."

"P . . . O . . . I . . . N . . ." The sergeant enunciated each letter as his pen scratched resolutely across the page. "And the address, sir?"

"Fourteen, Holmwood."

Nearly half a minute went by. Mrs Pointer, in the next bedroom, was making quavering sounds of distress in her sleep. "Oh, shut up!" muttered her husband under his breath.

He heard Worple's satisfied "Um" indicate that the address had been safely stowed. Then "You said something about an explosion, sir. Perhaps you can describe it?"

6

"Of course I can't describe it. It was a bang. It woke me up."

Worple remained silent a moment. "So what you mean, sir, is that you believe an explosion occurred while you were asleep but that you didn't actually hear it." He smiled at Pointer's gurgle of exasperation and stretched one leg. "Is that what you wish to report, sir?"

"Look here, I didn't ring you up in the middle of the night to quibble about forms of words. For all I know it might have been a gas main blowing up. People's lives might be in danger." His annoyance invested this spontaneous hypothesis with realism: God, we might all die in our beds for anything these cloddish policemen would stir themselves to do.

"That isn't very likely, sir, if you'll forgive my saying so," came the patient voice from Fen Street. "You see, coal gas – the ordinary stuff you get when you turn a tap – is largely hydrogen and it only becomes explosive when it's mixed with the oxygen in the air we breathe. And gas mains, as a general rule, are enclosed. Air doesn't get into gas mains, sir."

"Or, for heaven's. . . ."

"But if you've reason to believe there is a fault in your supply, you're quite right to report it, sir, even at this time of night. Would you like me to give you the number of the Gas Board escapes department?" Worple smirked tenderly at the apple he had begun to polish upon the jersey beneath his unbuttoned tunic.

The furious Pointer said nothing more, but slammed the receiver down and stood clenching and unclenching his hands. Hearing another querulous little wail from the next room, he went softly to his wife's door, opened it wide, and heaved it shut again as hard as he could. His scowl blossomed into a grin as he listened to the hoots of terror within.

A minute later, he affected a noisy and cross awakening when Amelia Pointer pattered to his bed and nervously touched his shoulder. "Ozzy," she whispered, "what was that?"

"What was what?" he snarled.

She fled, squeaking apologies, out of the room.

On his way to his warehouse in the morning, Pointer overtook a neighbour, Barrington Hoole, who was sauntering slowly towards town and the optician's shop which professional dignity did not allow him to open one minute earlier than ten o'clock.

Hoole confirmed that a detonation of some kind had shaken the district during the night and added the polite hope that it had not been Mr Pointer's own personal bomb going off "after all these years".

The reference was to an unconfessed but famous prank in the winter of 1942, when a quite unwarranted "Danger: Unexploded Bomb" notice had appeared overnight outside Pointer's off-licence and ruined his Christmas trade.

Pointer ignored the reminder of this misfortune and said some harsh things about the indifference of the police to pubic-spirited inquiries. Hoole nodded agreement while he strolled alongside, happily sniffing the June air and saluting, with benign superiority, such of his fellow citizens as happened to be at their doors and dispensing those misleadingly affable salutations that are customary in small country towns.

The optician was a short, apple-cheeked man. His plumpness seemed to consist of compressed energy that he was at pains to keep from being transformed into unseemly haste or excitement. He had a femininely smooth chin, tucked well in, a beakish nose pinched at the bridge by new old-fashioned rimless glasses, an unlined expanse of intelligent forehead, and sparse but primly disciplined hair. His almost permanent smile might have been that of a man slightly mad, yet supremely fastidious in his eccentricity. Unlettered locals deeply respected Mr Hoole's air of donnish self-confidence, but they were suspicious and resentful of what they termed his "sarky" sense of humour.

On the topic of explosions, Pointer found his companion somewhat unresponsive, and the subject had been abandoned by the time they emerged from East Street into the fan-shaped area of Great Market. This green-centred triangle, containing a bus stand and a maze of cattle pens, was dominated by Chalmsbury's war memorial (commemorative of 1914-18 only; an addendum relative to the more recent conflict was still the subject of somewhat acrimonious argument in the Town Council). It consisted of a short oval column, set upon a plinth, and bearing the bronze figure of a heavily moustached infantry officer in the act, apparently, of hurling a pair of binoculars at the Post Office.

At the further end of Great Market, Pointer entered his office, leaving Hoole to pursue a leisurely course through Church Street, now tight as a gut with vans and trucks and cars and droves of seemingly immortal cyclists, across St Luke's Square and over the Borough Bridge to Watergate Street. Here were his consulting rooms, as he called the cupboard-like quarters squeezed between a furniture store and the melancholy mock-magnificence of the Rialto Cinema.

Looking at some stills outside the picture house was a big, loose-legged man in a brown, chalk-striped suit. His hands, clasped behind him, looked like a pair of courting Flamborough crabs. The back of his neck had the colour and texture of peeled salami.

Hearing Hoole's key in the shop door, the man turned.

"Hello there, Sawdust."

Hoole did not look round immediately. He knew who

9

stood there. Only one person in Chalmsbury delighted still to use the epithet earned long years ago at the Grammar School by the boy Hoole's shameful propensity for being sick in class and requiring the attendance of the caretaker with his bucket of sawdust and his deep, contemptuous sighs. Stanley Biggadyke, his chief tormentor at that time, had a memory crammed like a schoolboy's pocket with revolting oddities and carefully preserved bits of ammunition.

"Morning, Big." Hoole had used the pause to quell a strong temptation to outdo the other's offensiveness. He held open the door and grinned a bland, unmeant welcome.

Biggadyke stepped past him and peered round the dark little box of a shop. "Somebody's pinched those glasses you did for me," he announced.

"Pinched them?"

"Well they've gone, anyway. I'll have to have another pair."

"Have you the prescription?"

Biggadyke gestured carelessly. "I've got nothing. I thought you kept all that sort of thing."

Hoole pulled out a drawer in a small filing cabinet and fingered quickly and delicately through cards. He eased one up. "You had those spectacles six years ago. I'll have to test your eyes again."

Biggadyke's mouth, which was normally kept hanging slightly open like a ventilator in the dark red heat of his complexion, shut and twisted. "Trust you to pile on the extras. All right, Sawdust, let's get on with it. I've been waiting half the morning for you already."

Hoole opened a door at the back of the shop and pre-ceded Biggadyke up a short flight of narrow, carpeted stairs to the room above. Other customers, he knew, would soon be arriving for appointments but they would have to wait. He couldn't trust himself to face a postponed encounter with Biggadyke in anything like his present state of self-control.

Calmly he switched on the lamps over his charts and padded around making preliminary adjustments to pieces of equipment that his patient eyed with sceptical amusement. "All part of the act, eh, old man?"

The optician hummed good-humouredly. When he was satisfied with his arrangements he motioned Biggadyke to sit in the padded, upright chair facing a mirror in which the charts, behind and above the chair were reflected.

The sound of a horn, strident and imperious, penetrated the quiet, shuttered room. Biggadyke raised his head and scowled. "That's my bloody car." He listened a while, then relaxed. "Kids. Carry on, Sawdust."

Hoole opened a small, glass-fronted case. "You can drive all right without glasses, then?"

"I can drive blindfold, cock."

Hoole grunted and sorted out a tiny brown bottle and a dropper from the contents of one of the shelves. "Hold your head well back and look to one side."

Biggadyke winced as Hoole let fall four or five drops of icy liquid into each red-rimmed eye. "Just blink them in," said Hoole. "They won't hurt."

"You didn't do this last time."

"It's better if I can take a good look inside. That's what this stuff is for. Keep your head back a few minutes."

Hoole had good reason to remember 'last time'. It was the only occasion – since his schooldays, at least – on which he had allowed himself to fall victim to one of Biggadyke's practical jokes. The town, he supposed, was still enjoying the story. A choice fragment of the Biggadyke legend. 'He's a card, old Stan; a proper rum 'un'. How rum could one get, Hoole asked himself. He glanced, almost apprehensively, at the reading chart. The four biggest letters that formed its top line were just as they ought to be: black, solid, meaningless. Not – his scalp tingled at the recollection – as they had unaccountably appeared to prim old Mrs Garside when she had taken the chair and been asked to read them immediately after Biggadyke's last visit to his consulting rooms. Hoole looked just once more to satisfy himself that Biggadyke had not again, in an unobserved moment, superimposed that frightful four-lettered word (cunningly hand-printed in reverse for mirrored presentation) upon the chart behind him.

Half an hour later Biggadyke strode from the shop, leaving Hoole, punctiliously professional, smiling in the doorway and holding against his waistcoat his lightly clasped, white little hands.

Before crossing to where a long, pale grey sports car was parked on the opposite side of the road, Biggadyke glanced quickly to left and right. He had begun to step out for the other pavement before realizing that there had been something odd about those glimpses of Watergate Street. He looked again to the right. Yes, the roadway seemed to bulge and shimmer. He blinked hard and looked up at the buildings. They appeared normal at first, then the horizontal lines of the roofs and parapets slowly sagged and blurred. And at the edge of every solid object there was an aura of intense violet light.

Biggadyke resolutely shut his eyes and shook his head. When he again peered around him, squinting past half lowered lids the view was more nearly in focus. He saw his car quite clearly – almost unnaturally clearly – in front of him. He reached for the door handle. To his surprise, he grasped nothing; he had to take fully two more steps before he could touch the car.

Feeling by now that mixed shame and alarm that the sudden failure of a physical function arouses in men normally robust, Biggadyke was at the same time aware of Hoole's responsibility for his condition and determined to deny him the satisfaction of seeing any evidence of it. He swung himself into the driving seat, started the engine, and, with a hideous tattoo of defiance from its exhausts, swung the big car into the centre of the road and aimed it as best he could on a mean course between the rows of curiously undulating shops.

He navigated the rest of the length of Watergate Street successfully, if only because it happened to be almost clear of traffic, the level crossing at its lower end having been closed a short time before. Only the Borough Bridge needed to be crossed; then he could turn off the square into the broad sanctuary of the White Hind's car park and rest until his sight returned to normal.

The car was on the bridge, moving slowly forward. Biggadyke knew that there would be a policeman on point duty where the bridge carriageway entered the square. He peered with painful concentration through the windscreen and searched among the luminous, lunging shapes ahead for one that might be a blue helmet.

He was still searching when an angry shout reached him from behind. Instinctively he glanced back. There the helmet was, bobbing in the intolerable glare of the sunshine.

In that instant, the front of the sports car folded before the massive radiator of a cattle truck and Biggadyke, flung like soft clay upon his admirable multi-dialled dashboard, closed his troublesome eyes and slept.

If the noise of the collision reached the ear of Mr Hoole, ministering to his second customer of the day in the quiet, softly lighted upper room, he gave no sign of being either disturbed or elated by whatever speculation it raised in his mind. "Head back just a fraction," he murmured. "That's fine." He delicately manipulated the dropper. One little globule fell neatly into the corner of each eye of the knowledgeable Mrs Courtney-Snell, who smiled and said: "Distending the pupil, eh, Mr Hoole?"

"Exactly!" replied Hoole admiringly. Mrs Courtney-Snell was not a National Health patient.

"Belladonna tincture," added Mrs Courtney-Snell. "And I'm not to worry if I cannot focus properly for an hour or two afterwards. The effect is disturbing but temporary. Isn't that so?"

"But how right you are! I can see that a mere occulist cannot pull any – ah – wool over your eyes, madam!"

Mrs Courtney-Snell condescendingly chuckled and settled back to enjoy a nice, long eye test.

In St Luke's Square the point duty policeman strode up to Biggadyke's car and wrenched open the door. At the sight of the collapsed driver he swallowed his wrath and sent the handiest intelligent looking citizen to telephone for an ambulance.

Biggadyke recovered consciousness before it arrived. He moaned a little, and swore a great deal. The policeman, bending down to make him as comfortable as possible on the pavement, surreptitiously sniffed his breath. It was innocent of alcohol.

"Mind you," he confided later to a colleague who had arrived to help, "it could have been drugs. Perhaps they'll know at the hospital when they take a look at him. I wish it had been the booze, though, like it was last time. He'd not have got away with it again."

The second policeman shook his head. "Don't be too sure of that, either. Big's got the luck of the devil. When they chucked out that case at the Assizes it was like giving a life-saving medal to a bloke who'd done in his granny."

"One thing; he didn't actually kill anyone this time," said the point duty man, and he stepped into the roadway to disperse once again the clot of inquisitive onlookers that threatened to dam what traffic could still trickle past Biggadyke's corrugated car.

He was not to know that killing was the theme of some

14

frank observations being made at that moment by Biggadyke himself as he lay in a small private ward of Chalmsbury General Hospital.

"There's a certain little gentleman in this town, duckie," he informed the plain young nurse whose cold fingers explored his wrist, "who'll be coming in here soon after I leave. But, by God, you'll have your work cut out to find *his* bloody pulse!"

The nurse frowned slightly and transferred her gaze from her watch to a corner of the ceiling. Her lips made tiny counting movements. Then she replaced Biggadyke's hand on the sheet with the air of a shopper rejecting a fly-blown joint. After stooping to write on the chart clipped to the foot of the bed, she stepped to the door.

"When are you coming back to keep me warm, nurse?" Biggadyke, even in distress, was sensitive to a situation's demands upon his virility.

The girl paused in the doorway, turned, and spoke for the first time since his arrival. "Please ring the bell if you wish to move your bowels."

2

THE NEWS OF STANLEY BIGGADYKE'S ACCIDENT WAS
borne to the *Chalmsbury Chronicle* office in Watergate
Street by the commissionaire of the Rialto, Mr Walter
Grope, in hope of some reciprocal favour, such as the
publication of his *Ode to St Luke's Church*.

Mr Grope had a large, harmless face like a feather
bolster. So loose and widely dispersed were his features that
he had difficulty in mustering them to bear witness to whatever emotion happened to possess him. His expression
either was spread very thinly, like an inadequate scraping
of butter over a huge teacake, or else clung in a piece to
one spot.

When he smiled, which he did seldom and with reluctance, the smile wriggled painfully from the corner of his
mouth, crawled a short way into the pale expanse of jowl,
and there died. His frown, though more readily produced –
for Mr Grope found life sad and perplexing – did not trespass beyond the very centre of his forehead. When he was
surprised, his eyebrows arched like old and emaciated cats.

So long as none of these extremes seized him, his face
registered blank bewilderment. He had only to stand for a
moment by the kerb for some kindly woman to take his
arm and try to escort him over the road. When he entered
a shop he would be assumed immediately to be the seeker
of a lost umbrella and assistants would shake their heads
at him before he could utter a word.

Yet in spite of his appearance Mr Grope had one remark-
able gift: the ability to rhyme at a tremendous rate. He

practised by mentally adding complementary lines to the remarks he overheard while marshalling patrons into his cinema.

Thus: "It's raining cats and dogs outside" (*So spake brave Marmion e'er he died*) or "Did you remember the toffees, dear?" (*Quoth Lancelot to Guinevere*) or "I liked that bit where Franchot Tone . . ." (*Ruptured himself and made great moan*).

This happy facility as a versifier enabled Grope to supplement the pittance he received from his employers. The arty-crafty trade, which flourished exceedingly in Chalmsbury, found him a great asset to poker-work production. Matchbox stands, trays for ladies' combings, egg-timer brackets – these bore such masterpieces of Mr Grope's as his *Ode to the River Chal as It Passes Between the Watercress Beds and the Mighty Oil-seed Mill*. To save the poker from growing cold too often the title had been condensed to *Ode* and only the first verse quoted:

> *The river winds and winds and winds*
> *Through scenery of many kinds.*
> *It passes townships and societies,*
> *And cattle breeds of all varieties;*
> *But even the river must surely stand still*
> *To admire our fine cress and Henderson's Mill!*

Upon smaller articles such as stud boxes, napkin rings and egg cosy identity discs appeared neat and edifying little slogans of Mr Grope's devising: *No Knife Cuts Like a Sharp Word* and *Mother – Home's Treasure* and *Remember Someone May Want to Use This After You*.

This being Wednesday and his morning free from supervising the Rialto's charwomen, Grope had walked abroad to contemplate man's inhumanity to man and to think up rhymes afresh. Having witnessed the collision in St Luke's Square and waited to see Biggadyke loaded into the ambulance he had retraced his steps as far as the cinema and crossed to the *Chronicle* office almost directly opposite.

Josiah Kebble, the paper's spherical editor, looked up from his desk on hearing Grope enter through the swing door. Between Kebble and his readers there was no other barrier. He considered the sociability of this arrangement well worth the occasional inconvenience of an outraged complainant bursting in upon him and demanding what he had meant by something or other.

"There's been an accident," announced Grope.

"Has there now?" said Kebble. "That's nice." He regarded Grope with amiable expectation and rolled a pencil between his palms. This produced a rhythmic clicking as the pencil struck against a thick, old-fashioned signet ring.

"That Biggadyke man has just driven into a lorry over in the Square. He's not dead, though."

"Stan Biggadyke, you mean? The haulage bloke?"

Grope nodded ruminatively. He thought *coke . . . soak . . . bespoke . . .*

"Harry!" the editor called. A flimsy door opened in a cubicle-like contraption in one corner of the room and a pale, startled face was thrust forth. "Can you spare a minute, old chap?" Kebble inquired of it, then, neither receiving nor seeming to expect an answer, he added : "Just nip down to the Square. There's been a smash."

The face disappeared and a moment later Harry slouched sadly through the office and out into the street, listing beneath the burden of a camera the size of a meat safe.

"Can't say I'm surprised, mind," said Kebble. He glanced at the clock. "I don't know, though. They're hardly open yet."

Grope, who had subsided thankfully into a chair, shook his head slowly. "It would have been a judgment," he said, "if he'd been taken. But his sort stays on, you know. I often wonder about it."

"A dreadful fellow, they tell me." Kebble said this in a tone almost of admiration.

"Ah..." Grope pondered. "He used to bring young women into the three and sixes. Marched them up the stairs like a drover. Mrs Parget said she never tore tickets for the same ones twice."

"Did he, er . . ."

"There's not a doubt of it. The usherettes got to be scared to use their torches. Think of that."

Kebble thought of that.

"He's not a patron any more," Grope went on.

"Really?"

"No. It's the television, I expect. Now there's an immoral invention, if you like."

The swing door thudded open and a lank-haired youth with nervous eyes and a red spike of a nose wheeled in a bicycle and propped it against the wall. "I've got a story, chief," he announced, gangling up to Kebble.

"Don't apply that loathsome expression to me, boy!" Kebble passed a hand through the daisy-white hair that sleeked straight back from his pink forehead and frowned like an abbot mistaken for a brothel keeper. "And next time you have occasion to ring me at the office please don't say 'Give me the desk.' Muriel thought you were a firm of furniture removers. Now then, have you got those church services?"

The youth, who was called Leonard Leaper, looked un-abashed. He struggled to extricate a large notebook from his jacket pocket and announced: "They've blown up the drinking fountain in the Jubilee Park."

"What are you talking about? Who's 'they'?" Kebble gave a sidelong glance at Grope, a recognized authority on calamities, but drew no response.

"They? Well, somebody. The perpetrators." Leaper looked pleased at this choice. "And every little bit of it's

19

gone. I've just been over to look. Some shrubs and things are down as well." He thumbed hastily through his notebook. "I interviewed the park keeper. He's married and has three children and he's an old boy of the Alderson Road School. He served in the artillery during the first world war and is a prominent member of the Royal Anti . . . Anti . . ." Leaper paused and peered at his shorthand with disbelief.

"Anti-vivisection?" suggested Grope, hopefully.

Kebble leaned forward. "Never mind that, Leonard. What about the explosion, or whatever it was?"

The youth reluctantly disengaged himself from the puzzle of what the park keeper was a prominent member of and turned over a page. "The outrage," he declared, "is thought to have taken place in the early hours of the morning. Mr Harding. . . ."

"Harding?"

"Yes, the park keeper. Mr Harding said that while sleeping at his place of residence in East Street he was awakened by what sounded like a big gun going off. He thought no more of the incident until, on his arrival at the park just prior to taking up his duties at nine o'clock, he saw a jet of water rising from the ground in the spot hitherto occupied by the drinking fountain. Of this edifice, a well-known land mark in the town. . . ."

"Hitherto," Kebble interjected.

". . . there was no trace." Leaper snapped shut the notebook and bent down to conceal his flush of triumph in the business of removing his bicycle clips.

Kebble looked at Grope. "What a very extraordinary thing. Who would want to demolish a drinking fountain?"

"Brewers," said Grope without hesitation. "They would do it. Any day of the week."

Kebble turned to Leaper. "Have you been round to the police?" The youth shook his head and began putting his bicycle clips on again.

"No, never mind. I'll give them a call myself." The editor stood and reached down a broad brimmed hat. "They might know something about Biggadyke by now." He nodded cheerfully to Grope, trotted round the counter and went out.

The police station was an integral part of the municipal buildings in Fen Street. This extravagant edifice, architecturally a compound of Baroque and Victorian wash-house, had two entrances. The main doors, leading to the rating, borough engineer's and town clerk's departments and to the council chamber on the upper floor, was reached by a flight of steps flanked by glazed tile walls in green, brown and ochre. On alternate steps were cemented cast iron pots from which sprouted cast iron plants, painted green and all very lifelike, save one that had been broken in the past and now bore on its main stem a gaspipe jacket secured by half-inch bolts.

At the side of the building was a less imposing entrance, a brown door permanently latched back in a small lobby from which an echoing white-tiled corridor led to the rooms and cells and dun-varnished court where Chalmsbury's contingent of the county police scurried at the bidding of Chief Inspector Hector Larch.

It was into the not very sympathetic ear of Larch that Kebble imparted Leaper's news of the destruction of the drinking fountain in Jubilee Park.

The chief inspector was an exceptionally tall man with a pasty angular face cradled within the rampart of his great lower jaw. While Kebble talked, he sat upright at his desk and gazed fixedly at an inkwell. He offered no interruptions but breathed through tightly set teeth, making a regular hissing noise that gave the impression of dutiful patience being gradually expelled by the pressure of annoyance within.

When Kebble had finished, Larch looked at him and

21

relaxed his mouth so that the hissing stopped. A cold smile replaced his frown and he spoke softly.

"You think the boy was telling the truth, or had someone been pulling his leg?" A faint lisp went with the smile.

"Oh, he's cretinous but not a liar," Kebble said, loyally. "Anyway, it should be simple enough to verify. I thought maybe you'd heard something already."

"Some sort of explosion was reported during the night from . . ." Larch turned over some papers on the desk. ". . . from Holmwood. Ozzy Pointer rang up about it, apparently. We've not had time to look into it yet."

"Well, that's the direction. Beyond East Street."

"Yes," said Larch placidly. He adjusted the already neatly arranged documents before him and added: "I suppose you want to make what you'd call a story out of it. A drinking fountain . . ." He smirked contemptuously. "You must be hard up. Come on, then, if that's what you want."

Quite suddenly, Kebble found himself following Larch out of his office and along the corridor to the rear yard. Larch climbed into his car, started the engine and drove with expert rapidity through the narrow archway into Fen Street before glancing stonily to see if Kebble had managed to scramble aboard.

When they arrived at the park Kebble again suffered the disadvantage of short legs as he tried to match Larch's striding progress between the bowling greens to where a group of curious and mostly elderly citizens had gathered around a jet of water.

Larch pushed brusquely into the ring. The damage was even more impressive than Leaper's account had suggested. Of the fountain's column, bowl, and graven inscription to the memory of the late Lieutenant-Colonel William Courtney-Snell, J.P., there remained no identifiable fragment. The surrounding concrete, now awash, was cracked

22

and deeply pitted. Some of the shrubs that once had formed a semi-circular screen were now leafless, as though stripped by an overnight winter; others had been blasted into stumps bearing a few tatters of bark.

One wooden wall of a small bowls pavilion about twenty yards away had been plucked out and thrown across the path. A row of bowls lockers behind it had collapsed, spilling their contents. These lay now among the debris like cannon balls in a stormed gun emplacement.

Kebble, who had removed his outsize hat not in awe but to facilitate his squeezing his head between the chief inspector and a particularly stubborn bystander, gave a soft whistle. "An outrage if ever I saw one," he remarked appreciatively.

The policeman grunted and gazed around over heads for someone who might profitably be questioned. At that moment Harding, the keeper, appeared through the park gates accompanied by a little man carrying a tool bag. Larch disengaged himself from the water-watchers and walked rapidly to meet them, followed by Kebble.

Harding halted before Larch and stared bitterly at the crowd. "A fine to-do-ment, this little old lot," he observed. His companion set down his bag, wiped his nose with the back of his hand and nodded agreement. Harding indicated him and explained: "From the water department. He's come to turn it off."

Larch ignored the introduction and the plumber, after grinning querulously at Kebble and shuffling a bit, picked up the tools and took himself off towards a small brick building on the far side of the park.

"You're Harding, aren't you?"

"That's right," replied the keeper guardedly; the chief inspector, he noticed, was looking airily over his head and he didn't like it.

"Just what has been going on here?"

Harding glowered. "Well, you can see for yourself. The fountain's gone. I don't know anything else about it."

"What were you doing during the night, Mr Harding?" Larch had the stance of an ascetic headmaster, listening abstractedly to the futile excuses of a boy caught chalking obscenities. But Harding was not to be intimidated. "Parachute jumping," he retorted.

The corner of Larch's mouth twitched but he continued to stare into space. "I really don't think that sort of attitude will get us anywhere, Mr Harding," he said gently, with his rustling lisp. "Just try and think, will you?"

"I was in bed, of course. What else should I have been doing?"

"You heard nothing?"

"I heard a damn great bang all right. A lot of other people did too, I expect."

"Did you think it came from the park here?"

"I didn't think anything. I went back to sleep."

"But when you arrived here for work . . ."

"I found this how-d'you-do." Harding jerked his head towards the outrage. Just then the water jet faltered, sank and disappeared. The plumber had located the stop-cock.

"You had the job of maintaining the fountain, I suppose : cleaning it, and so on?"

"That's right."

"Bit of a nuisance, was it?"

Harding blew out his cheeks. "Here, what do you think you're getting at?" He stared belligerently at Larch, then looked across at Kebble, as if challenging him to translate the innuendo into plainer terms. But Kebble was busy examining a cigarette he had just lighted.

Larch said smoothly : "It's entirely up to you, Mr Harding, to decide what you think I mean. I don't think I have said anything to which you should take exception."

"You as good as said I'd blown the damn thing up myself to save cleaning it."

For the first time in the interview Larch looked directly at the park keeper. "Really, Mr Harding," he said reprovingly. Then he turned and regarded the few ancients who still lingered around the site of the explosion. "I'd be obliged if you could find a few stakes and rope that area off. We shall want to take a closer look at it without being trampled to death by the Over-Sixty clubs."

As they drove back into town, Kebble said: "You don't really think he did it, do you?"

Larch smiled. "Why not? He's a cheeky bastard." With effortless precision he swung the big car out to the crown of the road and overtook a slow procession of vans and lorries. "Unless, of course," he added, "you know who's responsible."

"Me, old chap?" Kebble affected the pained surprise that he knew Larch expected of him.

"Certainly. But I was forgetting – a journalist never gives away the source of his information, does he?"

"Never," Kebble cheerfully confirmed. He found the strain of playing to Larch's humour did not diminish with the years.

As the car approached the Borough Bridge he was reminded of the other matter he had intended to mention. "You knew Stan Biggadyke had piled his car up, I suppose?"

"Has he really?" Larch sounded as if he had been told that the Great Lama had hairs in his nostrils.

"Didn't anyone tell you?"

"Maybe. What special reason have you to be interested?"

God, thought Kebble, here we go again. He said: "I'm interested in everything and everybody. A professional nosey parker. Squalid, isn't it?"

"You're a damned interfering old nuisance." Larch remained silent for a while, as he always did after a vitu-

perative remark so as to give opportunity for it to be wondered at and worried over. Then, quietly and with the
calculated indifference of a man fond of fancying himself
much feared, he went on: "Yes, I know about Biggadyke.
He was taken slightly ill when he was driving. He hit a
lorry. I believe he's likely to be in hospital for a day or
two. That's all."

"No charge?"

Larch gave Kebble a quick, angry glance. "Why should
there be?"

"I just wondered."

Drawing the car to the curb outside the *Chronicle* office,
Larch leaned across his passenger and opened the door.
Then he jocularly punched flat the editor's hat and handed
it to him. "Don't forget it's the police ball on the 14th.
If you give it a respectable mention this week I might
cancel the instruction I'm just about to give for you to be
booted out of the station next time you try and bother me."

From the pavement, Kebble acknowledged the sally with
a patient grin as he restored the dignity of his hat and set
it once more on the back of his head. Thoughtfully, he
watched the big car accelerate towards the Fen Street
junction.

3

SHORTLY AFTER LARCH HAD SAT DOWN AGAIN AT his desk, Councillor Pointer looked round the door. Larch beckoned him in.

Pointer sat down carefully and placed his bowler hat, brim uppermost, between his feet. He looked sour enough for this arrangement to have been a precaution.

Larch rested his jaw on his palm and regarded him lazily. "Now then, what's bitten you?"

"I was just about blown out of bed last night. I rang down here to find what had happened."

"Well?"

"The clot who answered couldn't grasp what I was talking about. He tried to tell me to ring the blasted gas board." Pointer's tiny black moustache quivered.

"He probably hadn't heard anything. Your place is a bit out of town."

"Don't be ridiculous, Hector. It rocked the street. You're not going to tell me you didn't hear it?"

"Not from Flaxborough, I didn't. Tuesday's my civil defence night."

Pointer grunted acknowledgment. "All the same, you can take my word for it; the windows nearly came in. And all that fool could do was to spell out my name letter by letter as if he was cutting it in granite. I want you to see he gets a kick up the backside."

Larch sighed. "Look, pop: we know all about that explosion. Sergeant Worple's over there now. It was Worple who took your report. Don't worry, he knows his stuff."

"Yes, but . . ."

"You're just in time for some coffee." Larch reached to a bell push at the side of the desk.

Pointer did not pursue the argument but his boot button eyes continued to pivot restlessly. He found singularly irritating his son-in-law's reluctance to admit the inefficiency of his staff.

"Are you calling in on Hilda later on?" Larch asked him.

"Possibly."

"Well you might tell her that Stan had an accident this morning. Nothing serious. Bent his wagon a bit."

Pointer's anger broke surface. "Biggadyke, you mean. Why that . . ."

"That's right," Larch interrupted smoothly. "He's in the General, I believe . . . Oh, Benson" – a squat, sandy-haired constable had appeared in the doorway – "make it two coffees, will you?" He waited until the door had closed, then looked at his visitor. "Why, what's Stan done wrong?"

"Just about everything he's ever had a chance to get away with. You know perfectly well what he is. It beats me why you let the swine into the house. As for allowing Hilda . . ."

Larch's long, sunken cheek twitched. "Yes?" he lisped.

"Well, damn it all, Hector . . ." Pointer glared at his hat, then suddenly picked it up and clapped it on the desk. The topmost of Larch's neatly stacked papers was fanned from the pile and floated to the floor.

Larch bent slowly and retrieved it. "Hilda's friends are her own affair, and when one of them happens to be a friend of mine as well so much the less need for you to worry. Or," he added after a pause, "her mother."

Pointer looked up at the ceiling. "Oh, for heaven's sake!"

"All right : I know she doesn't like him."

"I don't care a rap who she likes. I'm giving you my opinion, not hers. Biggadyke's not the sort of specimen I should have thought a policeman would care to associate with."

"You'd be surprised if I told you some of the people I have to keep on my social register. They'd be cut dead in the mayor's parlour but they're damned useful to me."

"That's different. I have to mix with some queer customers in my trade, but I don't invite them home if I can help it. Always keep 'em the other side of the counter, son."

Larch felt like telling his father-in-law that this, his advice-to-my-men manner, did not wash outside the committee room of the Comrades of the Trenches Club. But his shrug was a dismissal of the subject. He never carried an argument beyond the stage at which his ultimate winning of it became problematical.

In Jubilee Park, Sergeant Worple paced slowly and in isolation around the enclosure roped off by Mr Harding. He contemptuously ignored the stares of those whom the spectacle of his apparent quarantine had drawn, like inquisitive badgers, from the Old Men's Shelter. He also affected not to hear the disrespectful remarks of two or three small boys who kept asking him the time.

During the previous half hour the sergeant had collected a lot of measurements, in the relevance of which he had no faith whatever, and also what few material clues – mostly twisted metal fragments – as he thought might testify to his zeal and perspicacity. These he had put in an envelope.

Worple was about to quit his compound when he was greeted by a man who, though grey-haired, stood apart from the solemn excursionists from the Old Men's Shelter.

The policeman strolled over and ducked beneath the rope.

"Sheep dog trials?" the man asked pleasantly.

"Actually," said Worple, "no, sir. Your guess is very wide. The talk is all of an explosion."

"My!"

"Look over there, Mr Payne." He pointed to the concrete apron from which the last vestiges of water were steaming off into the midday sunshine. "We have reason to believe that that was the work of a bomb."

"Wasn't there a sort of memorial there? I seem to remember one."

"A drinking fountain, Mr Payne. An amenity. One pressed a button in the centre of the representation of a lion's face – its nose, as it were – and a stream of water was released downward from a faucet. It worked on the principle of mains pressure."

"Ingenious," remarked Mr Payne. He drummed his cheek with two fingers and stared thoughtfully at the space vacated by the drinking fountain.

Cornelius Payne bore a striking resemblance to the late Arturo Toscanini – not that the fact was much remarked upon in Chalmsbury. He had a triangular, sensitive face; crisp hair that tended to bunch at the sides; dark but by no means mournful eyes, deep set and watchful; and a waxed moustache that emphasized the firm, slightly sceptical set of his mouth.

The two men turned and strolled slowly toward the park gates. It was very hot and to the scent of drying grass mowings the light breeze added the oily tang of tar, spreading in wrinkled waves beneath the roadside dust.

When they were a safe distance from the eyes of the old men, Worple brought out from his tunic pocket the envelope of clues. He invited Payne to look inside. "That's about all I managed to find," he explained. "Of course, a mine detector's what you want on a job like that. You wear headphones, you know, and they give a sort of high-pitched squeal when the detector passes over metal."

Payne peered politely at the collection of mangled bits and pieces.

"They all mean something, looked at properly," urged the sergeant.

Payne gingerly extracted one of the objects and held it on his palm. "Try interpreting this," he invited.

The sergeant regarded it with head inclined first one way then the other. Finally he said: "Part of the firing mechanism, I shouldn't wonder, sir. Of the bomb, you know. That hinge, you see, would enable contact to be made when . . ."

"It's a suspender," said Payne. He dropped it back in the envelope.

Some minutes later when they were walking along East Street (it was regarded in Chalmsbury as no great reflection upon either party for a policeman and a civilian to be seen in companionship) Worple returned to the subject.

"I believe you're right about that thing being a memorial. I remember now. It was subscribed – paid for, you know – by Mrs Courtney-Snell."

Payne nodded. "Leather-chops. That's right."

Worple gave him a reproachful glance. "She's a magistrate, sir."

"Ah!"

"Yes, indeed. A Justice of the Peace. Now I wonder if anyone had a grudge against her. Or against her late husband, for that matter. He was a decent enough gentleman, though, as far as I recall."

"Wasn't he mixed up in a law-suit or something just before he died?"

"Not mixed up exactly," the sergeant corrected. "He was the successful plaintiff. He sued that haulage contractor, Mr Biggadyke, for slander. That's defamation of character by word of mouth, sir."

"A somewhat impetuous man, Mr Biggadyke, by all accounts."

"Very likely. But that was no excuse for him going

round and telling everybody that story about the Colonel and Bessie Egan."

"Ah, yes. And the spurs."

Worple shook his head gloomily and turned his attention to the mussel boats that were slipping in slow procession beneath the Borough Bridge, bound for the stages another quarter of a mile up river. "Tide time," he remarked, with the countryman's instinct for allowing no merely human speculations to interfere with the conscientious marking off of nature's periods.

"I suppose," added Worple, "that you'll be off for your dinner now. Think of me, won't you: straight off nights and being kept out of bed by this bomb business." The words were belied by his air of self-congratulation; obviously he found the bomb business a welcome diversion.

"Rotten luck," said Payne, watching for a chance to cross the road.

"Of course, you know what the trouble is," confided the sergeant closely. "It's the chief inspector. He hasn't the first idea when it comes to looking into something unusual. He's not had the education, you know. Still, keep that to yourself."

"I shall indeed. Naturally." Payne raised his hand in farewell and stepped from the kerb.

He did not, however, go straight to lunch. Outside the Nelson and Emma he encountered Barrington Hoole.

Wordlessly, as if by treaty, both men stepped down into the cool stone passageway of the inn. They pushed past the arguing overflow of farmers and seed merchants from the great bow-windowed market bar and entered the comparatively deserted tap room.

Seated in a corner was Mr Kebble, diligently writing on the backs of envelopes a platitudinous confection that he hoped would pass muster as that week's "Pew and Pulpit", a feature normally contributed by a rota of local clergymen, the copy for which had been lost in the case-room.

Taking a hasty swig from his tankard of brandy and water, the editor spotted the new arrivals and beamed. "With you in a minute." Then he penned, with the ease of long practice, three final unexceptionable sentiments, measured at a glance the total column-inchage, and thankfully screwed on the cap of his pen. "God bless us, every one," he murmured and swept the envelopes into his pocket.

This action seemed to serve as a reminder. He delved into another pocket and withdrew a still damp print which he put down on the table before Payne and Hoole.

The optician pinched his lips and hummed nasally a little tune as he appraised the photograph. "I ought to know this ostentatious projectile." He looked up. "It's Biggadyke's, isn't it?"

Kebble nodded. "Look at the depth of focus," he said enthusiastically. "Dead sharp."

"What happened to Biggadyke, then?" Payne asked.

Kepple leaned towards him and pointed to parts of the picture. "He's got every dent, has Harry. Every scratch. Look at that."

"Yes, but what happened?" Payne repeated.

"Hit a lorry – you can't touch the old focal-plane half-plate jobs. Heavy, but . . . God, see that fellow's foot near the back wheel? You could count the stitches in his socks."

"I trust the lorry driver escaped injury," said Hoole, anxiously.

Kebble wrenched his gaze from Harry's achievement and picked up his tankard. "Oh yes, he's perfectly alright."

"What about Biggadyke, though?" Payne persisted.

"In hospital, they tell me." He drank, then shook his head and frowned. "Those nurses must have a pretty rotten life."

Hoole stared out of the window. In the gap between two

warehouses a mast came briefly into view. "Tide time," he dutifully observed.

Payne broke the silence that followed. "Didn't I," he asked Kebble, "see you in Jubilee Park this morning? With a policeman?"

"You did, old chap. I didn't know you were there. That fellow Larch swoops about so. It's like keeping up with someone on stilts. I say" – he poked his face forward and looked suddenly earnest – "who do you reckon did it?"

"Did what?" Hoole asked.

As Kebble described the outrage Hoole's tight, smooth face gleamed with high amusement. "Oh God, the Snell cenotaph! Does she know? – No, of course she can't; she was in my place just this morning."

The editor grinned. "Once she does you'll not see poor old Larch off the chain until he manages to arrest somebody."

"That shouldn't give him much difficulty," said Payne. "Hasn't Joe Mulvaney confessed yet?"

"Must have done," said Hoole. "Unless he hasn't heard about it."

"Grope will have told him by now," Kebble said.

"Well, then."

The editor shook his head. "No, Joe's been overdoing it lately. Claiming those Leicestershire stranglings was a bit too brown. Right out of his district."

The trio prolonged the joke a little longer. None really believed that Joseph Terence Alloysius Mulvaney, cinema projectionist and slightly weak-minded victim of a sacrifice compulsion, would take credit for the Jubilee Park affair. It was just that he, together with versifying Grope and genially promiscuous Bess Egan and Edward Summerbine, fit-thrower, and Mavis Baggley, kleptomaniacal housekeeper of the town's probation officer, and several more, were familiar bent coins in the social currency. They kept

34

turning up among the loose change of conversation: droll reminders of life's sportive possibilities.

Yet oddly enough, just as the talk in the Nelson and Emma had reverted to that morning's road accident and Hoole was yielding to the temptation to tell a story about belladonna tincture, Mulvaney was doing precisely what had been so lightly predicted.

He was confessing, and to Chief Inspector Larch in person.

Larch had summoned the determined self-accuser into his office partly to deprive his staff of an opportunity for wasting time. But he had another reason. Like many of his kind, he allowed to percolate through his dislike of humanity in general a sentimental sympathy for freaks. He would allow Mulvaney to perform his act of sacrifice without the depressing indignity of conforming to a sceptical sergeant's dictation speed.

Mulvaney, who had never recovered from the experience, in the first week of his apprenticeship, of seeing "The Informer" screened, sat hunched in his chair and scowled with pale obstinacy at Black-and-Tan Larch. In spite of the heat, he wore a long, tightly belted raincoat and kept his hands in its pockets.

"Sure and I don't care if me poor body's full of English bullets this night," he was saying with a whining lilt that Larch found strangely soporific, "but not a word of treachery you'll drag out of me. Haven't I told you what happened, now? There was meself in it only, and that's the holy truth."

"You've not said why you did it, Mulvaney."

Scorn blazed suddenly in Mulvaney's big, gentle eyes. "Is it seriously you're asking me that? You'll be telling me next you've never heard of the annexation of Ireland!"

"Oh, of course," Larch acknowledged.

"Or of the Organization? Let's see if you'll say you've never heard of the Organization?"

35

Larch let this irony pass.

Mulvaney stood up. He clicked his heels. "Very well; I'm ready." He closed his eyes and added: "I suppose there'll be a farce of a trial?"

The Chief Inspector also stood. "Er, no," he said. "I can't say that there will."

A pained smile flickered over Mulvaney's face. "Ah, yes. So it's the cellar and the car's backfire you'll be having in mind, captain?"

Larch came round his desk, walked to the door and opened it. Mulvaney continued to stand blindly at attention. Then, hearing Larch cough, he opened his eyes.

He stared at the doorway, gave a quick, bitter laugh, and strolled carelessly towards the proffered freedom. "Ha! It's the ambush, is it, after all?"

Larch nodded as he passed. "I'm afraid so. The cellar's being re-decorated."

4

THE OBLITERATION OF THE COURTNEY-SNELL
memorial had no significant sequel for two weeks. It was
reported, at considerable length and with biographies of
everyone who could be remotely associated with it, in the
following Friday's issue of the *Chalmsbury Chronicle*.
Police inquiries proceeded, of course, or were said to. Mrs
Courtney-Snell quivered and threatened and enjoyed the
solicitude of her peers. And small children in Jubilee Park
went thirsty. That was all.

It was agreed to have been a queer affair, but not unduly
alarming. As a topic it fell quickly to grade three.

And then, during the night of Tuesday, 17th June, there
was a second explosion in Chalmsbury.

Councillor Pointer did not hear this one. It occurred more
than a mile from his red brick villa in Holmwood and was
not particularly loud, anyway. So Sergeant Worple's
successor on night duty remained undisturbed by the
telephone and was able to leave the Occurrence Book ful-
filling its proper function as a door stop.

The next morning two women happened to step
simultaneously out of the front doors of their adjoining
houses in Chapel Terrace. She who failed, by a split second,
to start speaking before the other stood staring stonily
across the road awaiting her chance to seize the con-
versational initiative. At first she gazed unseeing, intent
only upon having ready a counter-stream of loquacity, but
after a while she became aware that something in her line
of vision was most curiously amiss. She grasped the second

37

woman's arm, shook her into silence, and exclaimed:
"Look – his head's gone!"

And so it had. Alderman Arnold Berry was no longer
regarding the wide world with that straining-at-stool
expression that denotes, in the convention of public
sculpture, a man of high but unpopular principles. He was
peering instead – or rather his head was – into a bed of
wallflowers.

"Whoever could have done that?"

"Those Mackenzie kids, I expect."

"Not that, they couldn't. It's metal."

"Here, do you know, I thought I heard something in the
night. . . ."

"A sort of slamming noise?"

"A bang. Just outside."

"That's right. It was."

"I wonder if. . . ."

"Well I never!"

And so the report eventually reached Chief Inspector
Larch that the statue of Alderman Berry had been
decapitated and that two residents of houses opposite the
railed courtyard in which the memorial stood had heard
an explosion during the night. He drove immediately to the
scene, accompanied by Worple.

The bronze figure had been transformed into something
a surrealist might have found eminently satisfying. The
spread hand of its down-reaching arm indicated the
recumbent head, as if in proud witness to a feat of strength.
The alderman's other hand, robbed of the cheek it had
supported in an attitude of pious bloody-mindedness, now
stuck erect in jaunty salute. The statue of the town's fore-
most temperance pioneer could not have been more
shockingly desecrated had a brazen beer barrel been
riveted between its feet.

Worple stared at the topped effigy for fully half a minute.

"It quite turns you up, doesn't it, sir?" he said at last.

"No," said Larch. He faced the other way, scowling at the houses that overlooked the chapel courtyard and searching his memory for the names of such of their occupants as had incurred his displeasure in the past.

The sergeant knelt and examined the head.

It appeared to have been cleanly fractured except for an area at the back of the neck where the metal was twisted and jagged. The charge must have been placed there, like a poultice. It had been enough merely to smash a smallish hole and to topple, rather than blast, the head from the trunk.

Worple stood and gave Larch his opinion, adding that explosions were funny things and he wouldn't rule out the possibility of damage coming to light further afield when a thorough search was made.

"Never mind that," retorted the chief inspector. "Just have a quick look round on the spot. There's someone over there I'm going to have a word with if he's in." He strode to the gates, crossed the road and knocked on one of the doors in the grey stone terrace.

Mr Grope, as it happened, was not in. He was playing his favourite role of bearer of strange tidings to the receptive Kebble.

His wife told Larch simply that he was down in the town and started to close the door.

"Just a moment, Mrs Grope. . . ."

She paused, regarding him suspiciously through weak, puckered-up eyes. "He's out. You'll have to come again."

"I am a police officer, Mrs Grope. Might I ask you a couple of questions?" The woman made no move and Larch added firmly: "Inside, if it wouldn't be too much trouble."

She turned, leaving the door open for him to follow. He caught up with her in a tiny, furniture-crammed parlour that smelled of old wardrobes. Without invitation, Larch seated himself in an arm-chair.

"I'd like you to tell me if you heard anything unusual during the night. Something like a firework going off, perhaps."

Mrs Grope shook her head. "I don't enjoy very good hearing," she explained huskily. "My hubby, now – he's very keen in the ear. He says he can hear the gentleman next door picking his nose." Her mouth dropped open to disclose toothless gums and Larch's face was fanned with short, noiseless exhalations. Mrs Grope was laughing.

The spasm stopped as suddenly as it began and she added: "That's just in the way of being one of his jokes, of course."

"Was your husband here in the house all last night?"

"Eh? Yes, where else would he be? There's nowhere to go when he gets back after the last house pictures."

"But if he had gone out again, you might not have known, might you, if your hearing's not too good?"

Mrs Grope looked blank. She sensed enmity.

"I do seem to remember, you know, Mrs Grope, that your husband took a night trip once before without your knowing anything about it."

She stared at the long, pallid face above the prow-like jaw. "How do you mean?"

"He was reported missing, wasn't he? We wasted quite a lot of time that night."

Mrs Grope gave an angry little puff. "Well fancy throwing that up again! You know very well that was all a mistake and no harm done." She patted the blouse over her thin chest and indignantly tugged her apron straight. "Anyway, if anyone was to blame it was Mr Biggadyke. He nearly lost father his job over that business."

The memory was not one that she cared to be revived, least of all by a coldly aggressive policeman who seemed intent on forcing her into association with some new unpleasantness that she knew nothing about.

The incident to which he referred had happened about two years before. Grope had awakened in the middle of the night, uncomfortably aware that he had neglected, for once, to search the back row of the circle before leaving. This was a moral duty that he imposed upon himself whenever Mr Biggadyke visited the cinema in consort. 'My ladies', as Grope termed the morning cleaners, deserved better, he considered, than to suffer the embarrassment of chancing upon evidence of Mr Biggadyke's diversions.

So Grope had arisen silently from his bed and had gone back to the picture house. But having repaired his lapse he inadvertently fell asleep again in one of the seats and remained there until the arrival of the charwomen some six hours later. It was then that he learned of the awakening of his wife, her descent downstairs and horrified discovery of what she took to be a suicide note on the dining-room table, and the subsequent hunt for his corpse by the half-dozen policemen whom Larch had managed to mobilize in grudging response to Mrs Grope's hysterics.

Mrs Grope, though not sharing her husband's addiction to rhyme, would never forget the couplet whose first line Grope had jotted down in a moment of sudden inspiration before leaving the house that night.

Weary of sights on earth, I'll stretch my neck,
To glimpse the clouds that Luke's high tower bedeck.

The second line, being still at the chewing over stage, had not been added. How foolish they had been made to look. And Mr Larch certainly had not believed the explanation. His present attitude showed he still thought Father had been deliberately having him on. You're spiteful, she said to herself; that's what you are, Mr Dishcloth-face.

Larch questioned her a little longer, but to no avail. She

was by now convinced that his sole design was her self-incrimination as a deceiver of policemen. The best defence was to know nothing about anything and this line she sourly maintained until Larch abandoned her parlour.

The chief inspector found Worple still perambulating slowly around the chapel courtyard, his head bowed. Now and then he halted, gently probed the gravel with his foot and bent to peer at it. In one hand he carried an envelope.

"I think we can get back now, sergeant," said Larch. "No use fooling round here all morning." He spotted the envelope. "What have you got there?"

Worple held it out to him, as if offering a toffee. "Odds and ends, sir. Like we collected in the park the other week."

Larch glanced into the envelope and eyed without much interest the bits of metal it contained. The only recognizable fragment was a tiny toothed wheel. "Might be anything," he said.

Worple folded the envelope and put it in his pocket. "That's so, sir. On the other hand, they might be" – he paused – "of forensic significance."

"What? Oh yes; quite." Larch had not caught Worple's undertone of reproof. He was looking up at the rapidly clouding sky. "Come on, man; it's going to rain." They hastened to the car as the first swollen drops smacked down.

Within ten minutes the late Alderman Berry's favourite beverage was fast filling his hollow legs.

Mr Kebble liked rain. It protracted and seemed to make more intimate, more productive of confidences, the visits of his friends and informants. On fine days they merely looked in to deliver the bare bones of a story, were content sometimes to toss them from the doorway. Kebble, like a fat but agile pug, caught them easily enough and expertly digested them, but he much preferred to make leisurely and careful selection from the offerings of callers who were not for ever looking at his clock and saying, 'Ah, well' or 'Good Lord!' Visitors marooned by the weather never behaved like this. They sat, as Mr Grope was sitting now, well back in their chairs and carelessly signalled time's winged chariot to overtake.

"It didn't exactly wake me, mind," Grope said. "Nothing ever wakes me. Only worry sometimes. Left over thoughts, you know – they lie like pastry. But I must have heard it, all the same. As soon as the better half came up with my breakfast this morning I sat up and said, 'There's been another one.' She knew what I meant and I was right."

Kebble nodded happily. News of the posthumous execution of Alderman Berry, whom he remembered as an incorrigible hand-shaker and tops for humility among the highly competitive penitents of the New Zion Brotherhood, had put him in an even better humour than usual.

"Do you reckon there's any connection?" he asked.

"Connection with what?"

"Why, that park business. The drinking fountain."

Grope considered. "It may very well be," he said after a while, "that both crimes were the work of the self-same . ." He searched for the word.

"Miscreant." This timely contribution came from Leonard Leaper, who was standing at one side of the editor's desk and following the conversation like a starving footman at a banquet.

Grope turned his sad eyes slowly towards the reporter. "I was talking to Mr Kebble," he said.

The editor waved Leaper to his own desk. "I'm still waiting for the Ferguson wedding. Did you collect the form?"

The youth held aloft a grubby sheet of paper.

"Good," said Kebble. "Write it. By the way, just

43

remember that for our purposes marriages are neither consummated or 'solomonized'. And for God's sake don't ever again describe the bridesmaids as wearing Dutch caps." He returned his attention to Grope.

"There was a film being shown to our patrons last week," the commissionaire resumed thoughtfully, "that was all about a man who was unjustly convicted of someone else's misdoings. And when he came out of prison he was an enemy of society and did a lot of dreadful things that were much worse than the one he had been sent to prison for not doing, if you follow me. There was some blowing up in it, I remember, and . . ." He lapsed into silence.

"Yes?" Kebble prompted.

"I don't know. I always had to leave at that part and check the ice cream trays. Mrs Hardacre in back stalls said she'd take it over on the Saturday but she must have forgotten because she didn't come out until it was time to put her harness on and then it was Coming Attractions."

"Oh dear," said Kebble politely.

"So you see the person I think the police ought to be looking for is someone here in the town who's been turned into an enemy of society – perhaps through being sent to prison for a crime he didn't commit."

"That ought to be a lot easier," Kebble daringly remarked, "than having to pick from all the people in Chalmsbury who *haven't* been sent to prison for things they *did* commit."

A tiny spot of pink appeared in the centre of Grope's vast dewlap. For a moment Kebble thought his visitor was going to look at the clock. He hastened to placate him. "You've an idea there, Walter. Somebody wanting to get his own back. A bit unbalanced, maybe."

Grope condescended to expand his theory. The wilful destruction of one monument and the marring of another indicated vengefulness, he thought, of a special kind. Both

44

the commemorated gentlemen had been magistrates. Did not this fact lend strength to his suggestion that the perpetrator was the brooding victim of a miscarriage of justice? In that case, it was to be expected that the object of the next outrage – if there were one – would be part of the same pattern. The representation of a magistrate, or another memorial to one. Was Kebble still with him? Yes; well, then.

The only targets of such a kind that survived in the town – and Grope had given the matter exhaustive consideration – were the portrait of Mrs Courtney-Snell in W.V.S. uniform that hung in the reading room of the public library (Kebble mentally rubbed his hands at the thought of the eclipse of this Gorgonian image) and the noted Chipchase tenor bell presented to St Luke's Church by William Chipchase, canning merchant, three years previously.

"Those are what we'll have to watch now," counselled Grope. "If he picks on one of those we'll know for certain the fellow's an ex-convict. That should give the police a very useful lead."

"You've taken the brewers off your list then, Walter?"

"Ah" – Grope raised a finger – "just a minute. You might think I was joking about that the other week. Being flippant, perhaps?"

"Not at all, old chap."

"No. Well listen. There does happen to be one other way of looking at this business. It might be the law that this man wants to get even with: we've considered that. Or it might" – Grope lowered his voice – "it might be that he's got a down on temperance!"

Kebble looked shocked.

Grope leaned forward very slightly in his chair. "Take the drinking fountain, now. Temperance – a perfect model of temperance. And now poor Arnold Berry. A magistrate, I grant you. But sobriety itself."

The editor pondered this paradox.

Grope sat back again and folded his hands. "It's quite simple," he said. "Whatever gets blown up next will tell us who the . . ." – his eye flickered to Leaper – "the miscreant is. The portrait or the bell: gaolbird. But a dairy or the Salvation Army barracks, or something of that kind: seek out the son of Bacchus."

"What a field that would offer," murmured Kebble.

This time Mr Grope really did look up at the clock. And he said: "Ah, well. . . ."

5

MR GROPE WAS NOT THE ONLY ONE WHO SOUGHT A connection between the two explosions. Leonard Leaper also gave the matter thought. His reasoning was conditioned by regular absorption of radiation from the *Daily Sun*.

This vital journal, the joining of whose staff was Leaper's idea of ultimate beatitude, had taught him that any two consecutive events that displayed the slightest similarity were a series. So he knew that what had disturbed Chalmsbury was a succession of crimes that promised the indefinite recurrence in headlines of phrases like 'strikes again'. This was satisfactory for, like all true devotees of the *Daily Sun*, Leaper cherished continuity and liked life's amazements to conform to established definitions.

Thus, although he would have dismissed as futile the subtle theorizing of Grope, he quickly spotted and approved the coincidence of both explosions having been set off on the same night of the week. The third, he was sure, would take place on a Tuesday also.

Tonight, perhaps: why not?

He had therefore prepared himself, if not for a probe, at least for a vigil.

Chalmsbury was not a large town and he calculated that an unobtrusive patrol of a few of its streets after midnight might easily enable him to catch sight of the dynamiter in time to stalk him to his objective. Optimism was another quality Leaper had acquired from the *Daily Sun*.

Before leaving his lodgings he dressed in dark flannels, a shirt and jersey of deep blue, and black plimsolls. He looked like a junior cat burglar.

His appearance was remarked upon as soon as he entered the Bay Tree snack bar in St Luke's Square where he intended to while away the time until it closed at eleven.

"I like your sleuthing set, Len."

He glowered at the round-faced girl who was shuffling along one of the table benches to make room for him. She giggled. "Where's the apashy hat?"

With great forbearance Leaper sat beside her and stirred the coffee he had collected at the counter. "I'm on a job," he announced.

"What, for the paper?" The girls eyes widened. "Is that why you're dressed up?"

"Gets cold towards morning." The casual tone bespoke veteran status in nocturnal news-gathering.

"What is it you're going to do? Tell me, Len."

"Depends."

"Are you on a story?" She pronounced the word as if naming a forbidden ecstasy.

He sipped his coffee and reflected that journalism's drudgery and humiliations had their occasional reward. He even permitted himself momentary enjoyment of a favourite vision: his nonchalant acceptance of a girl's All, eagerly bestowed in tribute to his having secured one of those scoops of the year that were featured every fortnight or so in the *Daily Sun*.

A glance at his companion, however, dispelled hope of the dream's imminent realization. Her eyes, engaged in another widening exercise, were fixed upon a new arrival. She shuffled her All towards Leaper, but not in tribute. It was to provide a seat for a young man wearing the splendid blazer of the Chalmsbury Co-operative Society Table Tennis Club.

48

Leaper moved to another bench. He drank very slowly a second and a third cup of coffee. No other girl spoke to him but he didn't care. Apart from that one recurrent fantasy in which his anonymous admirer ("Grateful Reader" perhaps?) disrobed while gazing at his picture and by-line, he regarded females solely as the elemental material of news stories. What matter if they snubbed him now? They would be delivered in time to his notebook, if not as young objects of Serious Offences or maturer victims of lust and ligature, then at last as pathetic shop-lifting matrons who knew not What Had Come Over Them.

This misogynist mood strong upon him, Leaper left the Bay Tree half an hour earlier than he had intended. He joined the aimlessly circulating stream of citizens, most of whom had just been disgorged from the nine pubs in the square, and were in that state of alcoholic optimism that forbids abandonment of the streets in case innkeepers should of a sudden discover their clocks to be an hour fast and re-open their doors.

Gradually the crowd thinned until there remained only three or four happy and demonstrative discussion groups. In a shadowed doorway Leaper looked and listened until these, too, dispersed. Then he crossed the square just as the cold, greenish purple veil of the mercury lighting was whisked from the sky and the moon's softer radiance flooded down.

Leaper halted by the corner of Friar Street and looked back. The tower of the parish church rode above the silvered roofs like a great stone horseman. It dwarfed even the most presumptuous buildings: the furniture repository that once had been a cinema, the four floors of Councillor Pointer's wine and spirits warehouse, the window-slotted concrete slab with which a national insurance company had sought to impress the natives. These and the rest of the shops and public-houses and offices had lost their

49

day-time identities. They looked as if they had bled to death.

Picking a route at random, Leaper entered Friar Street and padded slowly as far as the next intersection. A clock struck the first quarter after midnight. He stood and peered along the gently curving street on his left. It was empty save for a large ragged dog that trailed fitfully from gutter to gutter. The dog raised its snout on sensing Leaper's arrival and loped away.

Leaper chose the right-hand road which led eventually to the quays above the town. He kept to its moon-shadowed side where the houses were tall and without front gardens. Further along, these gave way to newer houses and the symmetry of a council estate began to assert itself. He neither saw nor heard anything that encouraged exploration in that direction so he struck off through a narrow crescent, passed beneath a railway bridge and arrived at a junction of five roads.

At its hub was a small traffic island, planted with flowers. Five benches, each commanding a view along a road, had been provided on the island for the benefit of such aged persons as were spry or rash enough to scuttle across the surrounding speedway.

On one of the benches someone was sitting now. Leaper noticed him too late to conceal his own presence and was much mortified to see the man beckon to him. It was Barrington Hoole.

"You're Kebble's boy," said Hoole, with the air of an entomologist naming a not very rare beetle. "Are you running away from your indentures?"

Leaper sniffed and looked sullen. "Beg pardon?"

The optician settled himself more comfortably against the back of the seat and studied him. "Off to sea, I suppose," he observed amiably.

"I'm on a job."

"Ah." Hoole turned his gaze to a lighted window in a

house on the opposite corner and began to hum softly. He seemed to have forgotten Kebble's boy.

Leaper felt that he was being underestimated. His annoyance turned suddenly to boldness. "What," he demanded, "are you doing out at this time, Mr Hoole?"

Hoole accepted the challenge without any sign of resentment. "My housekeeper's on the prowl," he said simply.

Leaper took several seconds to digest this. Then he wiped the end of his sharp nose with a nervous flick of knuckles and asked: "Do you mean she's mixed up with this bomb business?"

"Of course not. She prowls at home, boy." He looked closely at his watch. "I usually give her a couple of hours to tire herself out and get back to bed. I could lock my bedroom door, but that would just encourage her."

"Does she prowl every night, Mr Hoole?"

"Good gracious, no. Once a month. Cyclical, you know."

"Like a loony?" Leaper, instructed by the *Daily Sun*, was well aware of the moon's influence upon those given to Striking Again.

"My housekeeper is perfectly sane," Hoole corrected him. "It is simply that she is amorously tidal, so to speak. But tell me" – he lowered his head suddenly and looked over his pince-nez – "what is this job you say you are doing? Has Kebble sent you?"

Leaper was not sure how much he ought to say to this man with a plump, polished face, benign but watchful eyes, and the upsetting habit of following up every observation with a little whinnying sound at the back of his nose. But he saw that he would have to give some account of himself or risk a complaint reaching his employer; Hoole, after all, was a friend of Mr Kebble. And perhaps the unlikely behaviour of his housekeeper was the true reason for his sitting on a traffic island at midnight. At least he did not appear to be carrying an infernal machine.

"I just thought I'd have a look round," Leaper said, "in case there was anything doing?"

"Doing?"

"Well, yes – anything out of the way. Sort of." The youth gestured helplessly.

Hoole leaned forward. "You believe you might meet our demolition expert: is that it?"

"I don't know," Leaper said, feeling suddenly apprehensive. Hoole's glasses, gleaming in the moonlight, hid whatever expression lay in his eyes. All Leaper could see was the smooth, sustained smile.

"Mmm," went Hoole, like a fat gnat. "Mmm . . . well, see you don't get into trouble, boy." He rose and pulled his waistcoat tidily over his paunch. "And don't go leaning up against any statues, will you?"

Leaper watched him cross the pavement and stroll off along a road that would lead him into East Street. He was tempted at first to follow, but baulked at the thought of being lured into a second encounter that night with the bland, yet oddly intimidating Mr Hoole.

While he hesitated and listened to the gentle, unhurried footsteps of the departing optician he heard another sound. It was the click of a front gate latch.

Moving round the island, he looked along the radial streets. The first two were empty. The third also seemed so, but as he was about to turn away he thought he noticed a movement twenty or thirty yards along. He stared at the spot and soon saw, a little further away, a shape detach itself from the darkness of a wall, cross a patch of moonlit pavement, and merge into the shadow beyond.

Leaper launched himself gratefully into the role of the silent pursuer.

Adopting a crouching half-run and almost brushing the walls and fences that gave him cover, he reduced the distance between himself and the other traveller on the long, straight street until he was able to slacken pace and keep about twenty yards behind.

Whoever it was he followed seemed to be taking care to walk quietly, but rather in consideration of the hour than in fear of being observed. He maintained short, steady steps and did not glance behind or to either side. He was short, of slim build, and swung only one arm. Beneath the other was a narrow case or package of some kind. Leaper wondered if it were primed.

Almost at the end of the street, where it became a lane serving only a sewage farm and a rose nursery, the small, purposeful figure turned to the right. Leaper reached the corner just in time to see it disappear through a narrow opening between a hedge and a high corrugated iron fence.

Leaper knew this fence; it surrounded the yard and transport bays of the Chalmsbury Carriage Company. The entrance, though, was further along; the path taken by his quarry merely skirted the fence. He could not think where it might lead, unless it was to the canal that cut through the fields about quarter of a mile away. Leaper did not greatly care for canals. They ran lovers' lanes a close second as the haunt of stranglers, slashers and assailants with staring eyes.

It was with slightly diminished enthusiasm, therefore, that he peeped round the hedge. The path, a cindered track bordered on one side by bushes and rank grass and flanked on the other by the iron fence, was deserted. He ventured a few yards along it and stopped to listen. A lorry engine rumbled spasmodically somewhere fairly close at hand; it probably was one being warmed up in the Carriage Company's garage. He went on, glancing warily at the bushes on his left.

About a hundred yards from the road, the fence turned off at a right angle. Here the path appeared to end before a wooden barrier. When he came closer Leaper found this was a stile. He looked over into the meadow beyond. In its far corner a grey rectangular shape stood out against the darkness of a group of trees.

Leaper clambered over the stile and made his way through the clinging, dew-soaked grass towards what he soon distinguished as a large trailer caravan. Light shone through the two curtained windows on its nearer side.

He walked slowly round the caravan, like a diver seeking signs of life in a stranded submarine.

It had five windows in all and behind one of them the curtain was not quite fully drawn. He stooped and edged himself below it. There were voices inside the caravan, but Leaper could make out no words. The murmurous exchange seemed to be between only two people. As he listened, it became increasingly desultory and indistinct.

Crouched against the smooth panelling, Leaper grew cramped and dispirited. If the trail he had picked up with such high hope half an hour previously was to end in nothing more dramatic than a goodnight chat between two invisible occupants of a caravan – harmless holidaymakers, probably – he might as well have gone home to bed. Perhaps this was not the Bombing Terror's night after all. Or could the person he had followed be a decoy, charged with drawing him away from the site chosen for number three in the outrage series? Not even Leaper's self-esteem could persuade him of this possibility.

He made up his mind at last that he would risk taking a look through the window. If he were spotted he could dash for cover in the copse at the foot of the field or else double back the way he had come and seek sanctuary in the Carriage Company's yard, where a few drivers or mechanics were bound to be at hand.

He straightened up until his head was level with the small square of glass and a little to one side of it. Then slowly he craned forward. Through the inch-wide curtain parting there came first into view a broad shelf on which were bottles and two glasses. A handbag lay beside an ashtray in which a crumpled half cigarette smouldered.

As these things passed out of his narrow field of vision, a chair entered it. On the chair was a scarf. Then, quite suddenly, the scarf disappeared beneath something else. Leaper decided this to be a jacket or short coat. He waited. A long, dark, flapping shape hit the back of the chair and fell into a heap on the floor. Leaper frowned. Trousers, his mother had always impressed upon him, should be folded even were the heavens to fall. He watched to see if the owner of these trousers would regret his impetuosity and pick them up again.

Instead, a very strange thing happened.

Following the same trajectory as the trousers, a small fawn bundle sailed before Leaper's eyes and unfurled in mid-air into two slim, translucent pennants that floated down to join the jacket.

At first, Leaper was dazed by this so wildly incongruous arrival of a pair of nylons. Then slowly he began to realize that in assuming the person he followed to be a man he had been deceived by scarf-bound hair, masculine jacket and slacks.

Once the truth dawned that he had only to move his head a couple of inches to glimpse some latter-day Salome at the sixth veil, his cautious reasoning died as a candle flame in the gust from a furnace. He thrust his face against the window with such avidity that his long nose threatened to snap, like a carrot, on the glass.

The woman stood in the centre of the floor, about three feet to Leaper's left. She seemed to be having difficulty with the fastening of her penultimate garment. Her back was towards the window and she was looking down over her left shoulder, apparently at the owner of the long and hairy arm that Leaper could discern in the lower corner of his view.

The arm was extended in an eagerly helpful attitude, but the woman remained just beyond its reach, frowning slightly as her fingers struggled with a strap.

She was not, in Leaper's estimation, a young woman. Her face was of the kind he was accustomed to seeing at doors when he sought funeral details: it was a married daughter's face.

Where had he seen her before? If only she were wearing a normal complement of clothing, he felt sure he would recognize her. As it was, the strange, shocking, but irresistable circumstance of near-nudity somehow rendered her anonymous.

Leaper's memory was not helped even by the full view of her features that was presented a moment later when, her brassiere having yielded at last, she spun round in a kind of triumphant abandonment and with a brisk, matter-of-fact peeling action, achieved that state which Leaper had wistfully seen advertised outside fairground booths as Beauty Unadorned.

The watcher, whose pressed-brawn visage against the glass had miraculously escaped the woman's notice, found the revelation an anti-climax. Marriage with the light on, he decided, would be rather awful. He stepped back from the window, feeling weak and sour.

The moon had set and Leaper's only guide back to the stile was the outline of the Carriage Company's iron stockade against the faint luminescence of the summer night sky.

As he climbed down to the path, he glanced once more at the caravan. It was in darkness now. His sense of guilt and dismay grew suddenly stronger. He knew that sooner or later he would meet the woman again: no two inhabitants of Chalmsbury could avoid communion for long, even if it were only as customers in the same shop or companions at a bus stop. In any case his conviction increased that she was someone he had seen fairly regularly in the past and taken for granted, perhaps as the wife of some local big-wig. Whatever sort of a fool would he make of himself on coming face to face with her again? Suppose she were a public figure whom he was liable to have to report or interview. He began mentally ransacking a file of female councillors, magistrates and committee members.

At this juncture, though, Leaper's uncharacteristically rapid course of thought was arrested. He stood still and stared at the point on the skyline where he had just seen a small flash of reflected light.

Two seconds later came the sound of the explosion.

In Leaper's ears, it was like the boom of the cannon that signals a prisoner's escape.

6

ONE OF BARRINGTON HOOLE'S MOST CHERISHED
possessions was a period piece among shop signs: a huge
double-sided representation in coloured glass of a human
eye. It was of the same shape as a tinned ham, though
three times as big, and had been suspended from a bracket
above the doorway of his consulting rooms since the early
days of his predecessor, no believer in professional retic-
ence, more than forty years before.

So awesome was this Cyclopean grotesque that it
promised to outlast every other piece of portable or break-
able property that Chalmsbury shopkeepers were rash
enough to leave on display after barring their doors. Youths
with catapults shunned it. Drunks veered to the opposite
side of the road rather than pass beneath it. Even the
pranksome bucks of Chalmsbury Rowing Club forebore
from trying to add the thing to their collection of trophies.

The great eye, fringed with artificial lashes the size of
liquorice sticks, had glared out from its brass frame for as
long as Chief Inspector Larch could remember. So when
Sergeant Worple came into his office to report that it had
vanished he said merely: "Go to hell" and pushed the
message out of his mind.

Worple stood patiently in front of the desk until Larch
raised his eyes again. Then he said: "Beg pardon, sir, but
it looks like another of these bombing affairs."

"What does?"

"The destruction of Mr Hoole's shop sign, sir."

"What are you talking about?"

"The glass part of the sign has disintegrated – split up, sir – into pieces like grains of sugar. They're underfoot for quite a way along Watergate Street. Crunchy, they are."

Larch laid down his pen and gave Worple a jaundiced scowl. "Crunchy," he repeated flatly.

"That is so, sir. Glass is a crystalline substance, as you may know, with a lot of internal stresses" – he illustrated the point by hooking his fingers and pulling them – "so it tends to shatter on receiving a blow. The more sudden and powerful the blow, the more pieces the glass will fly into. An explosive, now. . . ."

"Never mind the bloody lecture. Who reported this?"

"Mr Hoole was the complainant, sir, but he didn't exactly report it. He just stood under where the sign had been and used bad language. I advised him to be careful and he changed to much longer words that didn't seem to give as much offence to bystanders. One of them told me it was the sign having been smashed that had upset Mr Hoole."

Larch rose, signed Worple to follow, and strode out of his office. A few minutes later they were looking up at the twisted remains of the framework that had contained the giant eye.

The chief inspector pounced into several shops nearby and promptly alienated their proprietors with aggressive questioning. One or two who lived above their premises said they had heard a loud bang during the night but they had no further information to offer and each plainly resented the implication that he was the author of the explosion.

Larch left Barrington Hoole himself until last.

The optician did not appear immediately but when he did descend from the upper floor he looked flushed and ready to lay tongue to more expletives of the kind he had been persuaded earlier to abandon. He nodded curtly at Larch and stood silent and challenging.

"I understand you've had a spot of trouble with your, er, advertisement out there, sir."

Hoole regarded him speechlessly for a moment then tightened his mouth and retorted: "Don't be fatuous, officer. You mean some blackguard blew the damn thing to smithereens. And just at the moment I happen to be in the middle of a consultation. You will have to pursue your inquiries elsewhere."

Larch swung his great jaw from side to side like a bulldozer seeking soft earth. "I wouldn't take too uncooperative an attitude if I were you, sir. The ownership of the advertisement doesn't give you the right to be indifferent to a police investigation, Mr Hoole. Blowing up property in a public place is a serious matter."

"Well you don't imagine I blew it up, do you?"

"In our job we imagine nothing, sir. We seek the facts."

"How you elicit facts without using imagination is your business, but it does help to explain your remarkably consistent lack of success."

"Did that sign thing of yours happen to be insured?" Larch inquired. His new description of the article in question lent itself to an even more contemptuous tone than he had succeeded in applying to 'advertisement'.

"Of course," said Hoole. "For thirty thousand pounds."

Larch looked wearily up at the ceiling. "Indeed, sir. In that case you must be exceedingly grateful that someone has enabled you to capitalize on the policy."

"Naturally."

"When did you leave your shop yesterday evening?"

"I left my consulting rooms at precisely five o-clock."

"And you didn't return until this morning?"

"No."

"You are certain of that?"

"Not absolutely. I am a schizophrenic, you know. Half of me takes a good deal of watching. Perhaps it slipped away in the night."

One side of Larch's mouth curled up like paper on a hot stove. "It strikes me, Mr Hoole, that both halves of you could do with watching." He reached for the door. "I may have further questions to ask you later."

"I gravely doubt if I shall have either the time or the inclination to answer them."

Larch opened the door, looked into the street, and turned back. "Ah, Mr Hoole," he sighed, "we have had our fun. But next time I shall bring a witness. And fun may then appear as obstruction and very wrongful."

Hoole put his finger tips on the counter, and leaned close to the chief inspector.

"May your truncheon take root in your orifice and become a thorn bush," he said with quiet sincerity.

Sweeping Worple into step beside him, Larch marched grimly back towards the police station. Worple, who had learned by now to keep a ready supply of envelopes in his tunic pocket, tried to explain on the way that he had performed his usual gleaning duty at the scene of explosion number three. But Larch waved down his report with some exasperation and the sergeant had to content himself with adding his latest collection of oddments to the two packets already lying between a tea caddy and a confiscated revolver in the charge-room cupboard.

When he re-entered his office, Larch found his father-in-law awaiting him.

"Now then, Pop," he said, with what pretence of cordiality he could summon at such short notice.

Councillor Pointer looked angry and unhappy. "There's been another, hasn't there?"

Larch sprawled in his chair and rubbed his jaw. "There has," he said, then, smiling slowly, "the best up to now."

"Never mind about that. Whoever's playing these damned tricks has got to be taught. The council will be furious. The whole town's. . . ."

". . . up in arms." Larch completed the councillor's favourite assertion.

"Well, so it is. I'm not joking. Can't you see what an impossible situation it puts me in? A chairman having to explain to his own committee that his own son-in-law hasn't been able to protect the town from a blasted bomb-throwing lunatic."

"He doesn't throw them, Pop."

"See here, Hector. . . ." Pointer paused and went on in a lower tone: "Have you honestly no idea of who's responsible?"

Larch did not reply at once. Pointer nodded. "So that's how it is."

"That's how what is?"

"Why did you hesitate just now?"

"I was trying to think what you were suggesting. Hadn't you better tell me?"

Pointer looked at the floor and began feeling aimlessly in his waistcoat pockets. "It's occurred to me," he said slowly, "and to more than one member of the committee that this sort of behaviour sounds remarkably character-istic of your friend Biggadyke." He looked up. "It does, you know."

"Why on earth should you think that?"

"Oh, don't bluster, Hector. You know what the fellow is. Anyone who could have fixed up that horrible contrap-tion in the Ladies at the Mayoress's At Home last year. . . ."

"That was never proved."

"We knew, all right. Biggadyke may look half-sloshed most of the time but he's an ingenious devil. What about that business of the hockey sticks at the High School? Don't pretend you had any doubt of who arranged that.

The fellow has a rotten streak right through. But just because he sponsored your membership of. . . ."

"l don't think you should say any more about that," Larch broke in. "This is all rather beside the point, anyway. Stan may have done some silly things in his time but I haven't the slightest reason to suspect him of this lot. I certainly wouldn't protect him, if that's what you're driving at."

"It wouldn't be the first time."

In the silence that followed, Pointer realized he had gone too far. Larch stared at him in cold fury. When he spoke, the words emerged like slips of snakeskin. "And what specific occasion had you in mind?"

The councillor shrugged uncomfortably. "If you must know, it was that driving case. People talked. As they will, you know. Things were never properly explained. Not the delay in a doctor turning up, at any rate."

"Go on."

"Well, it was said you'd given Biggadyke the chance to sober up before he could be examined."

"He asked for his own doctor. That was his right."

"His own man was away on holiday."

"We weren't to know that."

"You could have found out in less than the two hours it took you to get somebody else."

Larch pulled forward a pile of papers and began looking through them. "All that's been gone over. Forget it." His eyes still on the sheet of typescript before him, he felt for his fountain pen and unscrewed the cap.

Pointer flushed. "All that black coffee was never 'gone over'," he blurted.

Larch's head jerked up. "What did you say?"

"The coffee you got Biggadyke to drink when you thought no one was looking. A whole flask full that Hilda had made for you."

63

"Where the hell did you get that story?"

"Never mind who told me. You ought to know by now that nothing can be kept quiet for long in a town like this."

"Do you believe it?"

Pointer looked at him intently. "I'm not sure. It wouldn't go any further if I did. But you needn't get the idea that I'm going to cover up for you if you insist on inviting more suspicion. At least you should have a go at Biggadyke and let it get around that you'd questioned him."

Larch considered. "I might," he said.

"Good. That's sensible. Of course" – Pointer stood up and stared at the hat band of his bowler – "I don't say the fellow's necessarily guilty. You might be able to write him off altogether."

To this, Larch said nothing.

"And Hector, I do seriously advise you not to see so much of him for a while. Not until this thing's settled. Tell him to give Hilda a miss, too."

"I think you might leave me just a little discretion."

"As you like. I wouldn't have said anything, except that you don't seem to realize what trouble you might be bringing on yourself. And the family."

"The family?"

"Well . . . Hilda. And me."

"And dear mother-in-law?"

Pointer gave a short, humourless laugh.

When he had gone, Larch remained for some time gazing blankly at the papers on his desk. Then he lifted the telephone and asked for the Chalmsbury Carriage Company.

Stanley Biggadyke accepted a seat in the chief inspector's office and grinned in turn at Larch and at Sergeant Worple, who sat in the attitude of an umpire a few feet from the side of the desk.

"You may be wondering," Larch began, "why I asked if

you would be good enough to come and see us, Mr Biggadyke." He turned his head slightly in the sergeant's direction as if to acknowledge his share in the proceedings.

"Well, actually . . ."

"The fact is," Larch smoothly resumed, "that I wished to ask you a few questions in connection with a routine inquiry we are making. I thought you would prefer the interview to take place here rather than in your own office where unnecessary speculation might be aroused."

"Oh yes. Sure." Biggadyke crossed his legs and nodded sagely.

"So we shall begin by stating what you doubtless know already, Mr Biggadyke: that on three Tuesday nights this month, including last night, there have been explosions in the town which severely damaged various pieces of property."

"Another one last night, eh? You don't say."

"Yes, sir. In Watergate Street. The others were in the Jubilee Park on June third and in the Zion Church courtyard on June seventeen. Nobody hurt, but that doesn't mean we should view these things less seriously."

"Of course not." Biggadyke rubbed a puce-coloured cheek and pouted virtuously.

"In the absence of information that might suggest the identity of the culprit," continued Larch, ponderously, "we are obliged at this stage to pay rather more attention to gossip than we should normally be inclined to do, and to question every person whose name has happened to be mentioned. Of course, you quite understand, Mr Biggadyke, that this implies no actual suspicion on our part. We wish merely to eliminate everyone who can give a reasonable account of himself. Routine, you know, sir."

Biggadyke's expression had turned a little fractious. "What's this about mentioning names?"

Larch raised a long, bony hand. "Now, Mr Biggadyke, no

particular accusations have been made by anybody. But these explosions were arranged very skilfully. You'll agree that not many local people have much in the way of technical knowledge. It's only natural that anyone like yourself, with engineering or electrical qualifications, should come to mind. We should like to eliminate you from our inquiries, that's all, sir."

Worple, who had never seen his chief in so conciliatory a mood, watched him with one eyebrow raised and slightly open mouth.

"All right," said Biggadyke, expansively. "Go ahead: eliminate me."

Larch smiled and leaned back in his chair. "I imagine I need only ask you to give some brief account of your whereabouts during the three nights in question, sir. I'm not requiring a formal statement. Just tell me confidentially; you're under no obligation, of course."

Worple shut his mouth, swallowed, and looked across at Biggadyke. The dark, blood-laden face was puckered in thought. The powerful shoulders were hunched and one hand was occupied in smoothing expensive suiting over a thigh like a young hog.

Suddenly, Biggadyke slapped his leg (Worple almost expected a squeal to result) and gave Larch a triumphant leer. "Tuesdays. They were all Tuesdays, weren't they? Well, I'm out of town every Tuesday night. You can ask the missus. Anyway, you should know that yourself, boy. It's club night over at Flax. I stay on at a pal's place afterwards. Bert Smiles. He'll tell you."

At the familiarity of 'boy' Larch frowned and glanced to see if Worple had noticed, but the sergeant's expression remained blank.

"Oh well, sir," he said heartily, "that seems absolutely satisfactory. You could hardly be in two places at once, could you?"

"Hardly," Biggadyke agreed. His tone conveyed the controlled surprise of a man who learns that he has just said the right thing.

"And if it should ever be necessary to check your statement, sir," said Larch, drawing a pad of paper towards him, "the club is . . ."

"The Trade and Haulage, St Anne's Place."

"Thank you, sir." Larch made a note. "And this Mr Smiles?"

"Herbert Smiles, Derwentvale, Pawley Road. Councillor Smiles, he is."

Larch nodded and wrote. "Of course, we shan't trouble the gentleman unless it really can't be avoided. You understand that, sir?"

"Oh, Bert wouldn't mind. I once stood . . ." Biggadyke realized just in time that mention of bail would not be apposite in the present circumstances, even though Mr Smiles had, in fact, narrowly escaped conviction. He therefore substituted, with clumsy jocularity, ". . . stood in for him at a wedding." The laughter with which he capped this extemporization sounded like an assault on stubborn nasal mucus.

Worple shivered. But he felt almost sure by now that the large, apoplectic-looking, unlovable Mr Biggadyke was not the malefactor they sought.

7

THE AFTERNOON SUNSHINE POURED INTO ST
Luke's Square and gilded the canvas awnings of the market
booths. Buying and selling seemed suspended. Jacketless
stallholders stood talking to one another or leaned against
the timber uprights and sipped from big mugs of tea. The
turmoil of market day had burned itself out. Those who
ambled still between the rows of booths glanced without
interest at the diminished mounds of fruit, the wilting
lettuces, and the few remaining honeycombs, dressed
chickens, milk cheeses, saucers of shellfish and other
delicacies that once would have been drastically marked
down 'to clear' at this time of day but which now could be
carted off in the backs of shooting brakes to enjoy
refrigerated immortality.

Only one man had refused to succumb to the general
apathy.

He was a giant clad in greasy flannels and sweat-stained
singlet who writhed and slithered around the inner circum-
ference of the crowd he had collected with hoarse promises
to bend a six-inch nail into an 'S' between his teeth. Clasp-
ing ham-sized hands, bound with clouts, before his mouth,
he reached the climax of his exercise in a series of leaping
convulsions that sent such quantities of blood to his upper
parts that his great rigid neck looked like an inverted fire
bucket. Then, panting hard and licking his thumb a great
many times, he unwrapped layer after layer of cloth
from his fist and triumphantly held aloft a nail-turned-meat-
hook.

"And would any gentleman," he challenged his listless spectators, "care to straighten it out again? Eh? Eh? Would you, sir?"

Leonard Leaper, to his intense embarrassment, found the transformed nail lying heavy in his hand. He smiled weakly, shook his head, and offered it back. But the giant, his breath regained, had jumped three feet out of Leaper's reach and was now holding up a small box in one hand and with the other was scornfully indicating the unwilling nail-bearer.

"Shall I tell you something?" he yelled. He tossed his head and hanks of sweaty hair flapped back across his scalp like razor strops. "Shall I?" He gazed slowly round the circle of sulky but expectant faces. He crouched, still pointing at Leaper, and reverently laid the little box on the ground before him. He closed his eyes.

"This lad," he whispered throatily, "lacks the greatest gift of providence. Strength. Power." He flexed his own gnarled oaks and went on: "The Egyptians had the secret. Oh, yes. Yes. They knew about the life-giving fluid that flows down from the cortical thorax, into the spine – here" – he jabbed a finger into the small of his back – "up to the brain and down, down again to the reproductive system." He looked very satisfied with this itinerary, but did not open his eyes. After a moment's silence, however, he did open his mouth and expelled the word "DOCTORS!" with a violence that sent the nearest of his audience staggering backward.

The giant rose to his feet, repeated "Doctors!" in an only slightly less stentorian tone, and went on: ". . . sit up there in Harley Street, taking hundreds of guineas for telling people just what I tell you now. That fluid from the cortical thorax . . ." – he spun round and pointed down at the box – "the Egyptians knew, oh, yes . . . that fluid" – he scanned the crowd until his eyes fell on Leaper again – "is dissipated at your peril! Once the level falls below here" – he snapped a hand round to between his shoulder blades – "the spinal passages begin to dry up, the cerebellum shrinks, the muscles atrophy . . ." Hunching his shoulders, he began slowly advancing upon the luckless Leaper. "Headaches!" he cried, slapping his own temples. "Liver!" He groped amidst his guts. "Stomach!" Four inches of vermilion tongue lolled out over his chin. "Constipation, backache, bad breath, sleeplessness, dizzy spells, pain behind the eyes, catarrh, bad teeth . . ." The dreadful recital, illustrated with gestures of increasing ferocity, brought foam welling from the corners of his mouth. Then, with dramatic suddenness, the catalogue ceased. Leaper felt upon his shoulder a fatherly pressure, as if a rhinoceros had leaned upon it. "Give it up, boy!" he heard. "For your own sake. Give it up!"

Leaper tore himself from the giant's grasp, ducked and pushed his way out of the crowd. He was too agitated to notice that Cornelius Payne, who had been standing nearby, helped him to escape by opening up a passage.

"Very humiliating for you," said Payne when they were clear.

Leaper looked up at him and blushed. "What did he have to pick on me for?" he murmured.

"He very unkindly used you as a sort of advertisement, I think. 'Before Taking', you know."

"I couldn't see what he was getting at." Leaper kept his face down as they walked slowly away.

"Huckster's cant, Mr Leaper," Payne assured him. "Don't take any notice of it."

Leaper glanced at him doubtfully. "I do get headaches sometimes," he confided.

"Who doesn't?"

"Are they really something to do with that . . . that fluid stuff he was talking about?"

Payne grinned. "My dear Mr Leaper, you may take my word that everything uttered by that preposterous acrobat was sheer unadulterated piffle. It was, honestly."

Leaper remained silent a while but when again he looked up his pinched features had brightened perceptibly. The novel and gratifying experience of hearing himself addressed, without irony, as 'Mister' was beginning to register. Here, he reflected, was someone who would never, never call him 'Kebble's boy'.

"I say, do you know anything about medicine and that?" His uncomfortable enthralment by cortical thoracic fluid was at an end, but he saw that Payne's face was of the distinguished, handsome, slightly sad sort that he associated with great surgeons. Perhaps he could be persuaded to talk of miracle drugs and wonder treatments (Leaper was currently worrying a good deal about what he fancied to be signs of impending hairiness of the palms).

Payne's answer was a disappointment, however. "No, I'm sorry," he said. "Chemistry was about the nearest field to medicine I ever grazed in. And that was quite a while ago."

They were passing a small mock-Tudor doorway bearing the legend 'Barbara's Buttery' and the scrawled, partly erased comment 'She's crumby, too.'

"Would you care for a cup of tea?" Payne inquired graciously. "Thanks very much," said Leaper. They climbed narrow stairs and entered, diffidently, the hag-ridden chamber above.

While they sipped from folk pottery and watched fat women demolish, by genteel but rapid nibbling, piles of tiny cakes, Payne asked his companion flattering questions about journalism and mended the ego torn by the pill-peddlar's insinuations. Then they eavesdropped upon the conversation at the next table, with Payne inserting casual remarks of his own that Leaper found very droll and worldly.

The three women who provided this entertainment were Mrs Coady, wife of the Vicar of Chalmsbury, Mrs Courtney-Snell and Mrs Amelia Pointer.

"I'm inclined to think," Mrs Coady was saying, "that it's some outsider who is responsible. These perfectly dreadful acts are so out of character with all the people we know here."

"Gangsterism!" exclaimed Mrs Courtney-Snell. The red leather upholstery of her face creased with disgust.

"I wouldn't say that exactly" – Mrs Coady's determination to see only the best in people prevented her from saying anything exactly – "but visitors can be very thoughtless at times. They have different standards, you know."

"Or none at all," observed Mrs Courtney-Snell acidly.

Mrs Coady selected the least attractive of the cakes and sliced it gently. "Some motorists – from the North of England, I understand – quite shocked my husband yesterday. He went into the church and found them trying to break into the font. They said they wanted water for their car."

Mrs Pointer broke her silence with a faint tut of incredulity, then lapsed again into mournful contemplation of the vicar's wife.

"So you see," went on Mrs Coady, "that there are people who see nothing wrong in destructive behaviour away from home. Tourists can be terribly heedless of local sensibilities. They have a sense of humour rather like that of the Vikings. We must try and understand them."

"All that concerns me," said Mrs Courtney-Snell, to whom Mrs. Pointer's gaze had switched expectantly, "is that somebody has smashed poor William's memorial and that the police have not done a single thing about it. It's absolutely disgusting."

Mrs Pointer sighed and looked back to Mrs Coady. She obliged with: "Perhaps it is better that the culprit should be left alone with his own conscience."

"He's being left alone to make more of his filthy bombs," retorted Mrs Courtney-Snell.

"Now, my dear . . ." Mrs Coady's smile of patient deprecation reminded Mrs Courtney-Snell that her selection for the chairmanship of the St Luke's Fete Committee was not yet a certainty; she said no more.

At that moment, a carefully groomed, self-possessed young woman who had been surveying the room from the doorway walked up and greeted Mrs Coady and her companions. Mrs Pointer she addressed as 'mother'.

Leaper looked as if he had just scalded his throat. He slewed round in his chair and hid his face from the new arrival. Payne glanced at him with concern.

"I'll have to get back to the office now," whispered Leaper between gulps of his remaining tea. "Mr Kebble will be waiting for me."

"Very well, Mr Leaper. Just as you wish." Payne rose gravely, picked up the bill and followed the bolting youth.

Outside the tea shop, Leaper assumed shambling normality once more. "I'm awfully sorry if I rushed you," he said, "but someone came in I didn't want to see me. I chased up a story about her," he added with a touch of pride.

"Ah!"

"Something pretty hot."

Payne raised his brows.

"I say, don't let on about this, will you, but it was the woman in that grey thing, the one who came up to the next table. I suppose you don't happen to know who she is?"

"I do, as a matter of fact. Why, don't you?"

"Oh, I've seen her before, but last time she looked sort of different and I haven't been able to think of her name since."

"Different?"

73

Leaper looked uncomfortable. "Well, yes. She hadn't ... hadn't any clothes on."

Payne blinked and grasped the neatly waxed end of his moustache. "My word, Mr Leaper, you must have a very interesting job."

"Oh, yes," agreed Leaper, lamely.

"If what you say is true – and of course I don't doubt your word – you have enjoyed the presumably rare privilege of sharing Chief Inspector Larch's view of matrimony."

"Larch? How do you mean?"

"Simply that it was his wife we saw just now. Hilda Larch. Daughter of Councillor Pointer. Her mother was sitting next to us."

"Oh, Lord!" Leaper groaned.

He told briefly of what he had seen the previous night. Payne listened with polite interest but he asked no questions.

"I wonder," said Leaper, "who the bloke was. I only saw his arm."

"The owner of the caravan, I expect."

"You wouldn't happen . . ."

"No idea. Sorry."

Parting from Payne outside the *Chronicle* office, Leaper thanked him clumsily but warmly – and with absolute sincerity – for his company and for the tea. The angular, morose youth had never before encountered an adult human being willing to bear with him for more than five minutes at a time and the experience had stirred him. Payne accepted his gratitude with neither embarrassment nor condescension, said he hoped he might see him again, and walked off towards the jeweller's shop which he had left, in confident expectation of no custom, in the charge of an amiable but moronic assistant.

Leaper did not enter the office immediately. He had noticed a small crowd on the opposite side of the road, so he crossed and joined it. On a pair of steps Sergeant Worple was precariously working with a hacksaw and pliers in order to remove what was left of Barrington Hoole's shop sign. Below him, Harry the photographer half knelt on the pavement and squinted through the view-finder of his mammoth camera. His object was to frame the sergeant's head, whether artistically or wantonly he alone knew, within the battered oval of brass that hung from one slowly yielding hinge.

Worple pretended to be unaware of Harry's contortions, but he took care not to make any funny faces so long as he felt within range of that lens. At last, the whirring rattle of the old shutter and an assortment of ejaculations from the bystanders told him that he had been 'taken'. He gave a business-like sniff and completed his task with a wrench that nearly toppled him from the ladder.

Mr Hoole received Worple in a friendly enough fashion when the sergeant carried the eye frame into the shop and set it upon the counter. "I'll just give you a receipt for this article, sir," said Worple, searching amongst his envelopes. "We shall have to take it away for a little while."

"You may keep it for ever, if you wish," Hoole said pleasantly.

"If decisions rested with me, sir, I'd have it sent to the forensic laboratory. The chief inspector doesn't go much for science, though. He says all criminals condemn themselves out of their own mouths."

At the end of five minutes Worple carefully put away his pen and handed Hoole his receipt for 'one optician's sign, damaged, formerly situate 23 Watergate Street'. Hoole put the slip into a drawer.

"I suppose," Worple said, "that the chief asked if you knew anything that might be helpful when he came in this morning?"

"He didn't, as a matter of fact."

"Oh!"

"He merely tried, in the clumsiest possible manner, to persuade me to condemn myself out of my own mouth."

Worple shook his head sadly. "I do wish he wouldn't take that line, sir. He doesn't mean to be offensive, but people aren't to know that."

"It must be very trying for you, sergeant."

"I wouldn't say that exactly, sir. It's just that I don't like to see policemen getting a name for being unintelligent. Not all of us are stupid, you know."

As if to prove this contention, Worple scraped his thumbnail over a portion of the framework and prised off a sticky fragment. "Adhesive tape," he remarked. "Now the forensic people could probably tell us a lot from that."

"Really?"

"Oh, yes. Where it was made. What batch it was in. Name of the chemist it was sent to. When. All that. Yes." He looked a little longer at the piece of tape, then rolled it into a ball between finger and thumb and flicked it away.

"Should you have done that?" inquired Hoole.

"The chief would never bother with it, sir. He takes a very straightforward attitude."

"He spurns empiricism?" ventured the optician.

"Mr Larch spurns everything, sir."

The sergeant put an arm through his load of scrap brass and slung it to his shoulder. He opened the shop door and looked up at the bracket from which the sign had been suspended.

"There's something I find a bit puzzling," said Worple. "I had to borrow a pair of steps to fetch this thing down. It must have been, oh, eight or nine feet above the pavement. Now how do you reckon our chap reached it?"

"Reached it?"

"To stick his bomb on it, sir. You saw me indicate a piece of adhesive tape. Adhere means to stick. That's how it was done, you know."

"A tall gentleman perhaps?"

Worple shook his head. "An ingenious theory, sir, but I can't call to mind anyone hereabouts who's over seven feet tall."

"True."

The sergeant considered the bracket a little longer, then asked: "Do you happen to know who occupies the premises immediately above your shop, sir?"

"Of course. They're mine."

"Somebody could have reached over from that window."

"I suppose he could – provided he had first got into my consulting room."

"Would that have been possible, sir?"

"Perfectly. The place isn't burglar-proof. There's a door and a window at the back. Probably open now. I don't know."

Worple looked at Hoole reprovingly. "Might I take a look at them?"

Amidst the anarchy of the optician's back room, the sergeant examined what was visible of the door and the window behind piles of cartons and loose packing. He reported that neither was fastened.

"Very insecure premises, if I may say so, Mr Hoole."

"Yes, but who would want to pinch a set of sight-testing charts, my dear fellow?"

Worple pondered this briefly.

"Perhaps another optician, sir? One not quite so well established."

8

RELUCTANTLY, MR GROPE ADMITTED TO MR KEBBLE
that Outrage Three had foxed him.

"There's no rhyme or reason in it," he complained. "Now
if that Hoole man were Temperance . . ." Grope gloomily
wagged his head. "He's not even on the bench."

"There go both your theories then, Walter. Hard lines,
old chap." Kebble voiced his sympathy with a briskness
that Grope found distasteful. "It's all very well for you,"
he grumbled. "Newspapers aren't concerned with right and
wrong. But I like to get the moral flavour settled."

"Nothing moral about blowing things up, surely?"

"You can't tell for certain. That memorial and the statue,
now: I'd have said those affairs were downright wicked.
But now the wind's changed a bit, as you might say. The
eye-glass fellow's a rum character. The police are over at
his place now. Did you know?"

"Yes, I sent Harry across to get a picture. Oh, by the
way . . ." The editor turned and reached down a filing tray
marked 'MEMS'. He selected a sheet of paper which he
passed to Grope. "Poetry's your department, Walter. What
do you make of that?"

Grope held the paper at arm's length, tucked in his chin
and focused down the line of his nose as if taking aim along
a harpoon. He read slowly and aloud:

> 'In memoriam.   July 1st
> The thirst that from the soul doth rise
> Doth ask a drink divine;

> *There'll be that dark parade*
> *Of tassels and of coaches soon –*
> *It's easy as a sign . . .'*

"Well," said Kebble, "does that mean anything to you?"

"No. Except that it's not proper poetry and it doesn't seem right for an 'In Memoriam'."

"You only think that because it's not one of yours, Walter."

There was some justice in Kebble's taunt. Mr Grope naturally resented trespass upon those local fields of poesy he had made his own. One was the souvenir trade. The other was the 'Mems' section of the *Chalmsbury Chronicle's* small advertisement pages.

Each week there appeared some three columns of rhymed manifestos commemorative of deaths in previous years. A regular reader of these would soon have detected that most of them consisted of permutations of a limited number of standard couplets. Thus, in a single issue the lament: *'Oh, Father dear, you're missed by all; e'en though your picture's on the wall'* might appear five or six times. But whereas in one case it would be followed by *'We never heard you say goodbye; but you had gone, and God knows why,'* another panegyric would proceed with *'You'd had enough, you needed rest; so never mind, you were one of the best.'*

The reason for identical sentiments being expressed in relation to so many totally unconnected passings was that Mr Grope had been commissioned by the newspaper to produce a once-and-for-all selection of about thirty couplets to cover every contingency. These were numbered and set out in black-bordered leaflets that incorporated an order form ('mark lines required here') and were posted, like wireless licence reminders, to every household shown by the advertising manager's records to have suffered a death twelve, twenty-four, or thirty-six months previously. A four-year lack of response won subsequent immunity from canvass.

Most of the bereaved, in fact, were eagerly responsive. Mr Grope's epitaphs were widely admired and a certain social distinction attached to the public proclamation of grief. Indeed, an element of competition had crept into the business. To commission a shorter 'In Memoriam' than a rival relative meant loss of face. The fear that Sister Edie and Family would spread themselves to ten lines prompted Brother Fred and All at Number Seven to order twelve. Then, quietly appraised of this state of affairs by the advertising manager, Daughter Marjorie and Little Norman would top the family score with fourteen.

Grope read again the message that compared so miserably with his own round, explicit verse.

" 'Drink divine'," he repeated. "Sounds more like a brewer's advertisement. You aren't going to print it, are you?"

"Naturally. It's paid for."

"Who brought it in?"

"Nobody. It came this morning by post. No name or address, but there was a postal order. We don't usually take them unless they're signed, but this seems harmless enough. I just wanted to know if you knew the quotation. We don't want to risk any double meanings."

Grope tried hard to discover some undertone that would disqualify the blackleg rhymster but failed. He said again that he thought the piece inappropriate. Then something stirred in his memory. "And I think I know why," he added quickly. "I believe it's out of some song or other. That's where I've heard it."

"A hymn, perhaps," suggested Kebble. He knew that the advertising manager would relinquish a pre-paid 'mem' as willingly as a leopard parting with a newly killed kid.

Grope shook his head. "A song," he affirmed. "A ballad or something. Nothing religious."

"Never mind; it doesn't look as if it can do any harm." Kebble slipped the sheet back into its tray.

Grope looked up at the ceiling. "It'll come back to me," he said. "I nearly had it just then." He inflated his large grey cheeks and blew out air with a low, tuneless soughing noise. Kebble thought of graveyards.

A sniff announced the presence of Leaper. He came round the counter and strolled to his desk. The editor regarded him over his glasses. "What are you looking knowing about?" he asked.

Leaper turned. "Sir?"

Kebble fancied for a moment that he had seen Leaper smile. He sat upright with a look of alarm. The impression faded, however, and he relaxed. "All right, boy; have you something to write up?"

"A few pars."

"Get on with them, then."

Leaper sat before his typewriter, wound in a piece of copy paper and after five minutes' reflection began to jab the keys. Grope looked up at the clock and said: "Ah, well." He hated the noise of typing, Leaper's above all: it sounded like sporadic small arms fire.

About half an hour after Grope's departure, Leaper collected his copy and silently presented it to Kebble. As the editor read it through, an expression compounded of incredulity and horror overspread his face. "And what," he hoarsely demanded at last, "is this supposed to be?"

"I thought it would be a good kick off for a sort of gossip feature," explained Leaper, unabashed. "Like Tom Trenchant." Mr Trenchant was the *Daily Sun's* premier boudoir scourer. "Inside stuff," Leaper added.

"You'll have me inside if you persist in putting this kind of thing on paper. Take it away and burn it."

Leaper stared. "Do you mean you're spiking it, sir?"

Sighing, Kebble spread the sheets before him and motioned Leaper to his side. "You see, Leonard," he said patiently, "on a local paper like ours we have to live with the people we write about. It does make a difference. Did you know that there are at least three shops here in Chalmsbury where you can still buy a horsewhip?"

"I've been careful about names."

"Yes, I see you have. But I'm not sure that " – Kebble moved a finger quickly down the typescript – "yes, 'socialite wife of police chief '– I'm not sure that identification is entirely ruled out there, old chap."

"You could cut out 'socialite'," suggested Leaper.

Kebble shuddered. "I should have done that in any case. It isn't the important point, though." He pushed his fingers through his hair. "Let me put it this way. Chief Inspector Larch is a nice helpful fellow but a little on the dour side. I can't imagine that he'd thank us for telling the town that his wife – how did you put it? – 'is to be seen at swank caravan parties, latest craze of the Chalmsbury Top Set'. What's that, anyway? Sounds like teeth."

"People are jolly glad to get into the Tom Trenchant column. And he doesn't tone anything down." Leaper paused and added: "Like I have." He sensed that his employer lacked the *Daily Sun's* admirable determination not to be gagged.

Kebble looked at him sharply. "Now what are you driving at?"

"Like I said, sir. I toned it down."

"In what way? I don't call a reference to . . . to 'hairy-armed mystery playboy' toning down."

"Well, I didn't write anything about her taking her clothes off."

"What!"

Leaper shuffled. Then he looked Kebble in the eye and

said defiantly: "I'm sorry now I hushed it up. Things like that ought to be exposed."

Kebble opened his mouth, shut it, and began carefully tearing Leaper's copy into small pieces. "Never," he said, when the last had fluttered into the waste paper basket, "never do that again." He breathed deeply and pondered the chance of Leaper's ever appreciating the enormity of libel. The odds against, he decided, were astronomical.

"Leonard . . . just tell me what happened. I'd rather like to know."

Leaper told him. By the time he had finished, Kebble was aglow and making little popping sounds. This disconcerted Leaper, who saw nothing amusing in a situation that his Fleet Street mentors would have treated with a proper blend of innuendo and self-righteousness.

"It's all quite true, sir," he protested.

Kebble raised a hand and pouted. "My dear boy, I don't doubt it for a minute. Hilda Larch was always a little unpredictable. Like her mother." He smiled fondly over his distended waistcoat, as if gazing down the years.

"You really don't want me to write anything, then?"

The editor gave a start. "My God, no! Not a word in writing. Listen . . ." – he pointed to the machine room door and lowered his voice – "they've only to see a bit of paper with words on that somebody's left about and they'll set it. I have to watch them like a hawk. I think they come back at night, foraging. Haven't you noticed the queer things that get in the paper sometimes? It was half a page of an old seed catalogue once. It had blown in from the street. The proof-reader should stop them, of course. But he's too frightened. They've got him at their mercy in that little box of his."

Leaper received the information in silence.

"So mind," Kebble wound up, "don't ever forget to clear

your desk before you go home, or Bullock and his bloody crew'll board it."

That evening there was a meeting of the General Purposes Committee of Chalmsbury Town Council.

Councillor Pointer was in the chair and he awaited with some apprehension a question that he knew was going to be asked under 'Any Other Business'.

It was Councillor Linnet, a truculent little man without teeth, who put it.

"Mr Chairman," he began, the wind of public-spirited purpose whistling through his gums, "everybody in the town is getting very alarmed and anxious about all these explosions. They're dastardly, Mr Chairman; there's no question about that. Now what I want to know is what is being done in regard to putting whoever's responsible under lock and key."

The brief speech won a murmur of approval. At least six of the ten members present had already discussed the matter among themselves in the card room of the Mariners' Club and decided on a vigorous joint bombardment of Chief Inspector Larch's father-in-law.

Trying to assess the probable strength of his enemies as he glanced quickly round the chamber, Pointer saw that he had no chance of frustrating them with an outright refusal to accept Linnet's question.

"I'm not sure," he said carefully, "that this committee is competent to discuss the matter, is it? The detection of crime is the province of the police."

Councillor Linnet was ready for this. "Come now, Mr Chairman," he retorted, "public safety is involved in regard to this. We may not be a watch committee but we have every right to chivvy the police if we think they're not being efficient in regard to protecting our rate-payers."

"How do you know whether the police investigations are proceeding efficiently or otherwise?"

Linnet gave the ceiling a 'hark-at-him' grin. "We don't need to have second sight to know that. There's not been an arrest in regard to this business. And there should have been by now. I want to know what the police are doing."

"The point with me, Mr Chairman," put in a venerable gentleman with a white quiff and a dewlap, Alderman Haskell by name, "is that these terrible bombs, or whatever they are, are going off on public property. You're quite right when you say it's a job for the police; we all know that. But these aren't what you might call private crimes. They're a danger to everybody, like road subsidence and rickety buildings and all that sort of thing. We as a committee can't just stand aside while the town's being blown to bits."

"We could," suggested Councillor Pointer, "ask the police to let us have a report. Confidentially, of course. Would that . . . er?" He looked from face to face. Alderman Haskell nodded and one or two others looked blank but the Linnet faction rumbled scepticism and its leader returned to the attack.

"No, Mr Chairman, I don't think it would. I have my reasons for saying that, mind, but I don't want to go further in regard to them while the Press is here. I'm going to move that we go into closed committee." Linnet looked across to where Mr Kebble was seated at a small table and made a not unfriendly grimace. Kebble acknowledged it with a wink and a curious two-fingered salutation from behind the shelter of his notebook.

"I second that," called out Councillor Roger Crispin. "Not," he added, "that I approve of 'Iron Curtain' tactics in this council, but I'm prepared to believe that Councillor Linnet has good grounds for wanting privacy."

There was a brief silence while the chairman looked

questioningly at each in turn of those members who could usually be depended upon to take the opposite line to anything sponsored by Messrs Linnet and Crispin. On this occasion they remained unresponsive.

"All those in favour?" Councillor Pointer asked tonelessly. There was a murmur of assent. He turned towards Mr Kebble and gave him a faint smile of dismissal.

Kebble pocketed his four pencils, picked up his notebook and made for the door. More than one of the watching committeemen felt something of the embarrassment of the after-dinner speaker who arrests the denouement of a dirty story during the slow departure of a waitress.

Then cigarettes and pipes were lighted, someone having noticed that nine o'clock had brought the expiry of the standing order against smoking. Councillor Linnet again addressed the chair.

"Now that we can speak plainly, I'll come straight to the point in regard to this bombing business. A whole lot of people have told me – they've stopped me in the street, rung me up at the shop, called at my home even – they've told me that they think the police here in Chalmsbury haven't made an arrest because somebody – I repeat, somebody – doesn't want an arrest. A certain name's been mentioned a good deal, but I don't propose to repeat it here. I think the chairman will have a fair idea of what I'm . . ."

"Oh, no, he hasn't," growled Pointer, "and I think you'd better explain that insinuation before you say any more."

Linnet rolled his head from side to side. "Now, Mr Chairman, don't go off with the idea that I'm getting at you personally. I'm trying to do my duty in regard to the public interest and if it's got to be said that Chief Inspector Larch is a member of your family, so to speak, then it's got to be said, that's all. I was only hoping that you might be in a special position to help us understand what's going on."

"There's no question of anything 'going on', as you put

it," Pointer, flushed with anger, glowered at his inquisitor. "My personal relationships are no concern of any member of this council and I think that this attempt to drag them into a distasteful and perfectly pointless argument is monstrous."

Some 'hear, hears' were heard.

Alderman Haskell had begun to make the cud-chewing motions that always showed when he was about to be statesmanlike. "The point with me, Mr Chairman," he announced, looking round at his colleagues, "is that nobody here wants to cast any reflection on your good self. Let us forget that our police chief happens to be related to you by marriage – a proper and, I trust, happy marriage. The fact remains that a dangerous criminal, perhaps a lunatic, is at large in the town and for nearly a month nothing seems to have been done about it."

He paused to champ ominously once or twice. "I have myself heard on good authority that the police have received a confession. Yet no one has been taken into custody. There are other rumours in the town, no less disturbing, but I do not think we should form any judgment upon them ourselves.

"What I do suggest – and I should like to propose it formally now – is that we appoint a small deputation to see the Chief Constable of the county and ask him to look into the whole affair in the light of the public disquiet it has aroused."

There were nods and hrrmphs of assent when Alderman Haskell sat back in his chair and stroked his large nose.

Further contributions were made but they consisted merely of the repetitive sentiments, truisms, irrelevancies and other exercises in the enjoyment of the sound of one's own voice that passed in Chalmsbury for debate. No one suggested an alternative to Alderman Haskell's resolution and it was ultimately carried with nicely calculated allowance for a drink in the adjoining Mason's Arms, where Mr Kebble had been quietly celebrating his expulsion for the past three-quarters of an hour.

Kebble very quickly learned and stored away for reference all that had been deemed too delicate for his ears. Then he drained the last of his brandy and water, guilelessly wished his informants good night, and set off for his office.

As he was walking past the Rialto, Mr Grope emerged to bolt back the doors in readiness for the nightly rush to dodge the national anthem.

"Ah, I was wondering if I might spot you," said Grope. "It's come to me."

Kebble pushed back his hat and looked sympathetic. "Has it, old chap?" Although he had no notion of what Grope was talking about he was conditioned to Chalmsbury conversation, which invariably began at the very point at which a previous exchange, however remote in time, had left off.

"That poem – it was a song; and so you see I wasn't wrong," intoned Grope. In mournful monotone he proved his point. "Drink to me o-o-only, wi-ith thine ey-ey-es . . ."

". . . And I'll not look for wine," responded Kebble. "Yes, of course. The first two lines of the 'Mem' follow straight on, don't they?"

Grope nodded and went on with his door bolting.

"But the rest of the thing – tassels and all that – I don't remember that coming into 'Drink to Me Only'. Why should . . ."

"Look out," said Grope. "Here they come."

9

THE DEPUTATION APPOINTED BY THE GENERAL
Purposes Committee to call upon the County Chief Constable consisted of three members. The choice of Alderman
Haskell was obvious enough. It was sanctified by his long
service, his patriarchal rectitude and his inability to recognize a can when one had been passed to him. He was
accompanied, for the sake of appearances and in order to
meet any legal snags that might be encountered, by the
Town Clerk, Mr L. C. Hooper-Dwyer. The third member –
none other than Councillor Pointer – had been selected
ostensibly by virtue of his chairmanship of the committee.
The real reason was his enemies' confidence that so heavily
compromised a spokesman could not fail to take the
opposite line to his personal inclination.

The trio was received by Mr Hessledine, the Chief Constable, with promptitude and affability. The good impression
made by this energetic attentive man in his neat grey suit
was strengthened by his remembering and using the name
of each of his visitors throughout the interview. 'Elsie'
Hooper-Dwyer expressed the general feeling when he
declared in the train on the homeward journey: "I do like
a gentleman who never calls you 'Er', don't you?"

Elsie it was who introduced the delicate subject of the
meeting.

"You will be aware, sir," he said, "of the disturbing and
inexplicable series of crimes which our community has
suffered during the past few weeks."

The Chief Constable nodded. "I have seen reports of the

incidents, Mr Hooper-Dwyer. I agree that they must have been most alarming." He was watching Elsie's face, which was intriguingly akin to that of a wax model in an old-fashioned hairdressing saloon: a smooth, translucent, flawless face that bore a silky little moustache. As the Town Clerk's precisely enunciated words popped forth, his little jaw was thrust forward to display a row of tiny, very white teeth. "How vicious he looks," thought Mr Hessledine.

After describing the bomb damage in somewhat tiresome detail, Elsie drew from his brief-case the minutes of the committee meeting and read a carefully condensed account of what members had had to say about the turning of blind eyes and the standing out of sore thumbs.

When he had come to the end of this document, he said: "Of course, I need hardly point out, Mr Chief Constable, that our reference today to the allegations is in the strictest confidence. Some of them may well be actionable. We quote them solely to give you an idea of public feeling, however unwisely you may think it has been expressed."

"I quite understand," replied Mr Hessledine. He paused for a few moments and said with a faint smile: "It all sounds rather sinister, doesn't it, gentlemen? One thing – your committee has been very sensible, I think, in deciding to be frank with us – with the police, I mean."

Councillor Pointer glanced up from a survey of his shoes to see the Chief Constable looking at him with polite concern. "Tell me, Mr Pointer, as the target of some of these unfortunate innuendoes, what do you feel about the affair? I must say, incidentally, that I much admire your courage in coming along here and taking the bull by the horns, so to speak."

Pointer gave no sign of being cheered by the compliment. "All I want," he said harshly, "is the scotching of these damnable rumours. Make what investigations you like. I've nothing to hide. Fire away and see if I care!"

"But I've no intention of firing at anybody, Mr Pointer. I was under the impression that you and your colleagues had come to fire at me."

Alderman Haskell champed portentously three times and spoke. "The point with me, Mr Chief Constable, is this. Chalmsbury, as you doubtless know is not a big town and the police have a very fair idea of who's who. In the ordinary way of wrong-doing, they never have much difficulty in putting their hands on the person responsible. Quite often someone will come along and tell them; we're quite neighbourly, you know. Well, we've certainly never before had the same trick played three times in a row and nobody under lock and key at the end of it."

"There must be a first time for everything," the Chief Constable observed.

"Yes and no," said the alderman, who tried always to see both sides of a question. "But be that as it may, our committee is far from satisfied that everything possible is being done in this case."

Elsie, who had been perched on the edge of his chair in readiness to extinguish with lawyer's qualifications any indiscretion that his companions might drop, shifted to a more comfortable position. "I think," he said, "that I should respectfully advise these gentlemen to regard their points as made and to elaborate no further. Unless, of course, the Chief Constable wishes to put any questions."

Giving him a little bow, Mr Hessledine glanced at a piece of paper on which he had been unobtrusively pencilling a few notes.

"There has been mention of a confession, gentlemen," he began. "That, I admit, is news to me. I shall have inquiries made, but I shall not be at all surprised to learn that my officers at Chalmsbury had good reason to ignore this confession, or whatever it was. Jokers and half-wits are forever giving themselves up for things that happen to have caught their imagination.

"The rest of what you say is rather more serious, isn't it?"

He folded his arms and looked briefly at each of the deputation. Then he swung his chair through a quarter turn, fixed his gaze on the ceiling and continued talking quietly, like a tutor recapitulating for the benefit of tiresomely zealous students.

"You naturally will understand that I cannot accept the implied criticism of Chief Inspector Larch and that my position obliges me to refute, in the absence of evidence, the suggestion that he has some ulterior motive for leaving this dynamiter of yours at large. I might reasonably feel very angry about what you have said, but I recognize that you are doing an official duty, as you and your colleagues see it, and also that these crimes must have put you all under a considerable strain.

"Now this is what I propose.

"Officially, I must send you away with a flea in your ear, so to speak. Unofficially, though, I shall do what I can to give our fellows over in Chalmsbury a little help in running this character to earth. You mustn't ask me to be more explicit, gentlemen. The less that's known, the more effective the help I have in mind will be."

This pleasantly mysterious undertaking having been won, the trio took leave. Even Councillor Pointer felt that things could have gone far worse.

When he was alone once more, the Chief Constable allowed his expression to lapse into something a good deal more like anxiety than he would have permitted his visitors to see. He stared moodily at the telephone, then suddenly picked it up and asked to speak to Mr Chubb on his private line.

Harcourt Chubb was the Chief Constable of Flaxborough,

the county town. He was a tall, ascetic-looking man who had scarcely ever been seen by his subordinates to sit down. This was not because he was energetic: his devotion to a quiet life was almost religious; but because he had learned that his insistence on standing in the seated presence of callers disheartened petitioners, frustrated complainants and generally reduced interviews to a minimum.

The system did not work over the telephone, of course.

"Harcourt! My dear fellow, how are you?" The County Chief Constable's swift injection of bonhomie left Mr Chubb paralysed, as though by a curare-tipped arrow.

"I'm in something of a fix, Harcourt. A very delicate matter, as it happens. . . . No, I'm sorry, it must be over the phone: I simply can't get round at the moment and things won't wait. Most of the explaining I'll do later, of course. . . . Yes, it would be nice to get together again. Dogs all well? . . . Fine. And Mrs Chubb? . . . Anyway, to get down to brass tacks I want to borrow one of your men for a spell. One who's unlikely to be known in Chalmsbury . . . Chalmsbury, yes. And I want someone a cut above those layabouts in dirty raincoats who can do nothing but harrass bookies for free bets. A real detective, old man. Now then, can you run to one?"

Mr Chubb explained icily that all his detectives were real.

"Naturally, my dear fellow. I was just pulling your leg. You know the man I want – cleared up that fearful brothel and butchery business of yours last year* . . . Purbright, yes, that's the chap. . . . Hard to say; two or three weeks possibly. Depends how lucky or good he is. . . . I say, that really is uncommonly obliging of you, Harcourt. . . . You will? Fine! And I'll tell you the whole story when we meet. Keep your powder dry, old man!"

Hessledine replaced the phone with a God-forgive-me

*Reported in *Coffin Scarcely Used*.

expression. The affectation of heartiness pained him a good deal, but he knew it was the only weapon to use upon Chubb, who would have parried any reasonably delivered request with courteous obtuseness and painstaking prevarication.

"Chief Inspector Larch? My name is Purbright. Flaxborough C.I.D. I expect the Chief Constable. . . ."

"Of course, Mr Purbright." Larch coldly appraised the man whose hand he shook. He was nearly as tall as himself, of slightly diffident manner and with a quick, apologetic smile. The fresh-complexioned face had a touch of foolish amiability about the mouth. Above grey eyes, steadily interested, it seemed, in what they saw, the high forehead was crowned with short but unruly hair of preposterous king-cup yellow.

"Yes, I'd heard you were being loaned to us in our distress." Larch resumed his seat and waved Purbright to another. "I only hope someone's told you what you're supposed to do. We" – he gestured largely with his hand – "are baffled."

"Perhaps the best arrangement," said Purbright, cheerfully ignoring the irony, "would be for me – the interloping damn nuisance – to be hived off where I shan't be always getting in your hair. The Chief's idea, apparently, is that my not being a local man might make me useful as a . . ." He shrugged; the suggestion had come out clumsily.

"As a Special Investigator," Larch maliciously provided.

"Sounds dreadful, doesn't it? Seriously, though, you don't want me cluttering up this place, do you. Let me go snooping in the open air." Purbright stared enviously at the sun-slaked pantiles of an old warehouse opposite the window.

"You are free to do what you please, Mr Purbright. I shouldn't be so childish as to try and make you feel un-

94

comfortable. You're only carrying out instructions – however goddam stupid I happen to think them."

"I was rather afraid that you'd kick me out."

"So I should if I thought you'd have any success in making me look small. But you're just wasting your time."

"Nothing could be a waste of time in weather like this." Purbright was still looking out of the window.

"All right. Make it a holiday. You might as well. Because this much I will tell you. The town's chock-a-block with lunatics. They'll chatter and natter for as long as you've a mind to listen. You'll get your criminal all right – a dozen times over. I only hope you've brought a cart."

Purbright smiled appreciatively. "Tell me, Mr Larch: what would be your own selected cart-load?"

"Oh, no. You've copies of the reports up to now. You go and play your own game."

"As you like. I was just showing a little friendly interest."

Larch regarded him narrowly, then grinned. "I'm a bit of a bastard, aren't I? Don't take it to heart, Mr Purbright." He reached for a folder at the side of the desk. "We'll go through them, shall we?

"My own favourite is a cocky, sarcastic little goggle-hawker called Hoole. You'll find his shop next to the Rialto. Unmarried; middle-aged but perky; likes taking the mickey – out of local institutions especially. Statues and memorials would be right up his alley. He's quite clever in his own way – academic honours and all that. Making bombs wouldn't present any great difficulty to him, I imagine."

"But hasn't this man's own shop been involved?"

"The oldest trick in the world. Self-inflicted injury." Larch leaned forward. "As a matter of fact, it wasn't terribly clever in this case. That sign was so high up that no one could have got at it without using a ladder or a chair or something. But it's quite accessible from Hoole's own upstairs window."

"Motive?"

Larch smirked derisively. "You don't want to worry about motives in this town, old son. There's just one that goes for the lot. Sheer bloodymindedness. Anyway, I've told you – Hoole's down on monuments."

"Right; who's next?"

"Joe Kebble. Editor of the local rag. He finds life a great bloody joke and I wouldn't put it past him to help the fun along a bit, especially if it provided him with some copy."

"Whoever's responsible would need explosive, I suppose. Is it sold hereabouts?"

Sparing this bland inquiry no more than a grunt, Larch went on with his suspect list. Mr Grope was on it. This was because of the opportunities for nocturnal villainy that his hours of employment afforded. Constant film-watching, moreover, might easily have put violent ideas into that great rhyme-rocked noggin.

Somewhat to Purbright's surprise, Councillor Pointer was included. "My father-in-law, if you must know," Larch frankly divulged. "I've nothing against him otherwise, nothing I can put my finger on, but he's hard to weigh up."

Purbright reflected that if everyone of whom this might be said qualified for investigation as a potential dynamiter he was going to need detention camps. Larch, however, had a more specific charge to level.

"Ozzy Pointer takes a long time and goes a long way round when he wants to do anybody but, by God, he does 'em in the end all right. Now for some reason or other he's taken a dislike to a chap in the town, a haulage contractor. I know him pretty well myself, as a matter of fact. He's settled down now but he used to be a bit on the wild side and the name's stuck. Pointer knows that and he's doing his damnedest to get the fellow knocked off for this bomb nonsense. I might add that Ozzy's word carries quite a bit of weight in this town."

"You mean you think that Mr Pointer has set the things himself?"

"To frame Stan. Yes, he could have done."

"Far-fetched, surely?"

"Far-fetched as hell, I know. But you see I also know that father-in-law of mine."

Larch remained silent while he picked a spot on the back of his neck. Then he slammed the file shut and growled: "Well, there you have it. Enjoy yourself. And if one of our home-smoked maniacs blows your own bloody head off, don't blame me."

10

ON THE FIRST OF JULY A BLOODY HEAD WAS BLOWN
off. But it was not Inspector Purbright's.

The day began inauspiciously enough with his removal
from the White Hind Hotel, where he had been ill-fed and
insulted by a staff who behaved like emigre dukes, to the
boarding house of Mrs Crispin.

It was one of the suspects who had recommended the
move. Treated to Purbright's account of his discomfiture
at the hands of autocratic porters, waiters and chamber-
maids at the White Hind, Kebble had shaken his head and
exclaimed: "Good God! You don't want to stay there, old
chap. Whoever put you on to that four-star pest house?"

Purbright loyally forbore from mentioning the advocacy
of Chief Inspector Larch and said he had just happened to
pick it because it was central.

"Get out," said Kebble, "quick. Now let me see . . . you
want to stay clear of all the hotels: there's not one I'd
quarantine a sick dog in. I'd put you up myself, but the
wife's got the loom working. . . ." He thought for a minute.
"Ah, I know. The chap's just left who was in with old
Payne. You'll be alright there, if she'll have you. Leonard
. . . take this gentleman round to Mrs Crispin's."

And Mrs Crispin, to whom Purbright presented himself
as plain Mister, did have him and gave every indication of
being delighted.

She was a woman of incredible girth, but the legs
beneath her capacious skirts must have been very short,
for she travelled as if on rails, with no vertical movement

whatever. Her face, which registered constant ecstasy in the presence of her 'gentlemen', was red and round under a black Japanese fringe. It was like the face of a rubber doll, enormously inflated.

Mrs Crispin having taken Purbright (metaphorically, he thanked God) to her gasometer-sized bosom, she detailed her help, Phyllis to escort him to his room and glided kitchenwards.

Purbright clambered breathlessly up three flights of stairs, marvelling at the ease with which the fine, farm-bred back and thighs of the girl with whom he tried to keep pace conquered the steep and angular ascent.

"Here you are, sir," she said at last, preceding him into a bedroom lined with varnished match-boarding and containing various tall, dark pieces of furniture that he was too exhausted to bother about identifying but which seemed to be awaiting him like chapel deacons, stiff with disapproval of a new communicant.

Phyllis set his heavy case on the bed with finger and thumb, gave him a quick but deeply dimpled smile, and departed.

Purbright sat and recovered his wind. Then he went to the narrow dormer window and, leaning on its sill, stared down at the little town where things had taken so unaccountably to going bump in the night.

He thought over his gleanings of the past couple of days: the readily offered accounts, guesses and insinuations, the terse police reports, the photographs and lists of times. They all boiled down to very little, perhaps no more than a series of eccentric pranks that had set off a chain reaction of parochial gossip.

Why, then, had Hessledine thought the affair worthy of special inquiries by an officer unconnected with the Chalmsbury Force? He had certainly not ordered them in response to representations by nervous civic dignitaries of whom he had said: "One end's so like t'other it's a wonder that when they take their hats off they're not run in for indecent exposure."

To only one confidence had he made Purbright partner. There had lately been reported missing from Flaxborough's Civil Defence training centre a quantity of explosives quite large enough to account for the incidents to date, with a handsome reserve for encores. "There may be no connection," the Chief Constable had said, "but the coincidence is far from happy."

He had not laboured the point. There was no need. Purbright was well aware that the leading light in the Tuesday evening demolition and heavy rescue course at Flaxborough was Chief Inspector Larch.

Purbright leaned out of the window and let fall a small and manly droplet of C.I.D. saliva upon the third of the basement steps below. The tiny smack it made was quite audible: sound was carried by the summer air as though it were strung with infinitely fine wires (later in the afternoon one would think to see them, glinting in the heat).

Larch, though . . . it was absurd. Each Tuesday he left for Flaxborough long before dusk and did not return until the following morning. All three bombs had exploded in public places; it seemed inconceivable that they could have been set in position during daylight.

What object could Larch have, anyway? He certainly gave the impression of being anti-social, but not to a maniacal degree.

A car came slowly along the street and stopped immediately below. It was a large, old-fashioned car. Through its retracted sunshine roof Purbright saw the driver lean forward and switch off the ignition. He got out of the car and entered the house. This, Purbright guessed, was his fellow lodger and doubtless a harbinger of lunch. He carefully made his way downstairs.

Mrs Crispin made introductions with the air of springing a joyous surprise. Then she stood back, beaming expectantly at each in turn. Purbright wondered if he were supposed to embrace this new blood brother, but Payne, accustomed to his landlady's transports, merely held out a hand and winked.

As soon as they were alone, however, he produced a minor surprise of his own "I must say, Inspector, that you don't look a bit like a policeman."

Purbright looked up from his soup analysis. "And who says I am a policeman?"

"Mrs Crispin. She's very proud to have acquired you."

"Indeed."

"You mean no one is supposed to know?"

"It really doesn't matter. I'm only a little disconcerted to find that one arrives in front of oneself, as it were. The communications system in this town must be excellent."

"First-rate," Payne agreed.

"And yet there are some things – quite well known facts, in all probability – that one simply cannot find out."

Payne raised his brows. "Really? But are you sure you've asked the right people? Even the most obliging can't help if they don't know the answers. The trouble with Chalmsbury is that no one wishes to seem unobliging. You'll always be given some sort of information, but the odds are that it will be wildly misleading."

"I see what you mean," Purbright said, "but I can't say that I draw much encouragement from it."

"Perhaps I can be more helpful. You are, I presume, following some specific line of inquiry here?"

"After a fashion."

"Police Probe Mystery Blasts?"

Purbright winced. "You really must not draw me into any indiscretions, Mr Payne."

"Indiscretions are currency in this town, Inspector. One

is traded for another. You must be prepared to start some-where."

"Is that my cue to ask whether I may trust you?"

"Nothing so banal. But as we are to share one of Mrs Crispin's cabinet puddings – today being Tuesday – we might as well recognize the bond of common tribulation and peril."

Purbright smiled. "Very well. Your guess – if it was only a guess – was perfectly correct. Blasts are what I probe."

Payne ate a while in silence. Then he said: "You will have heard already, or noticed yourself, that there is a pattern about these things."

"A regularity."

"That is so. Cabinet pudding is not the only feature peculiar to Tuesdays."

"One Tuesday, the second one, produced nothing."

"Why, I wonder."

"The gap may not be significant. Perhaps there happened to be no opportunity."

"Or perhaps our bombardier was otherwise engaged – detained, even."

"Quite." Purbright poured water for them both. "And what is your occupation, Mr Payne? No one," he added, "intercepted me on the stairs to tell me."

"I am a shopkeeper."

"How odd," said Purbright after appearing to give the reply some thought.

"Odd?"

"I'm sorry: I didn't mean to sound rude, but the term shopkeeper is so seldom used now. Scarcely ever by shop-keepers themselves. They seem to consider it derogatory and prefer to be known as provision merchants or shoe repairers or confectioners."

"In that case I suppose I should claim to be a jeweller. It's a pretentious description, though, for one who merely wraps up manufactured articles and passes them over a counter."

"Is that all that's entailed?"

"Virtually. I keep a shop: that's the sum of it. A parasitic existence, but it harms no one."

"You may not appreciate," said Purbright, "how precious that apparently negative virtue has become in these days."

Payne smiled and they talked of other things until the arrival of the cabinet pudding.

Where would the fourth bomb explode?

No one doubted that a bomb would go off. And Tuesday having been established as 'fuse-day' in the public mind by the phrase-coiners of Fleet Street, location was all that remained to be guessed.

Chief Inspector Larch grudgingly ordered special measures. Day duties were reduced to a minimum so that as many men as possible might be switched to patrolling after dark. They were told to concentrate on the main town area and to pay particular attention to such obtrusive features as statues. The chief inspector expressed regret that his Civil Defence duties in Flaxborough precluded his personal supervision of the precautions. He emphasised, however, that were he to find on his return that they had failed in their object, the life of his menials would cease to be worth bloody well living.

There was one serious flaw in Larch's plan. He had failed to realize that a considerable number of citizens would regard the occasion as a treat rather than an ordeal. So when all the carefully saved policemen were dispatched upon their appointed beats at lighting-up time they entered upon streets already crowded as if for a carnival. The closing of the pubs not only added to the number of spectators but instilled a recklessly jocular mood. There were shouts of "When's the rocket going up?" and one group in Great Market began chanting, "Ten, nine, eight, seven...." The policemen, who had been led to expect that the town would soon be deserted save for themselves and the prowling dynamiter, whose apprehending would therefore be a simple matter of challenge and chase, instead found themselves jostled, ironically hailed, and pushed by sheer weight of numbers from the path of duty. A hundred saboteurs, they bitterly reflected, could have concealed themselves in such a throng.

Shunning these scenes of excitement, with their flavour of an *auto da fe*, a youth in sleuthing suit worked his way round by side streets to the northern outskirts of the town and sought the fence-flanked path that led to a remembered stile.

Leonard Leaper had waged and won a short tussle with his conscience earlier in the evening. His first intention on changing into dark clothes and soft shoes had been the same as the week before: to discover, outwit and expose the criminal. Almost immediately, however, a sense of the unlikelihood of success flooded coldly over him and left him helplessly receptive to a much less creditable idea. The fact was that he had forgotten the revulsion that events in the caravan had initially aroused in him; it had been replaced by a lively desire to attend a second performance.

On arriving at the stile, he peered down the field. The windows of the caravan were dark. He cautiously approached through the grass. No sound came from inside. He tried to remember at what time he had arrived behind Mrs Larch the previous week. It must have been at least half an hour later than this – perhaps an hour, even. There was no need yet to conclude that his second excursion was to be fruitless.

Leaper walked slowly round the caravan, looking through the windows. There was still enough light in the western sky for him to distinguish the shape of objects inside: a chair, a small stove, the shelf on which he had seen the drinks and the handbag. Something was lying on the shelf now, something of about the shape and size of a boot box.

When he reached the forward end of the caravan, Leaper noticed a break in the window. His instinct for the dramatic told him that so small a hole – it was about four inches in diameter – in so large a pane of glass could have been caused only by a projectile. He received the daunting image of another secret observer, less fortunate than himself, spotted by the hairy-armed philanderer and promptly shot.

Leaper glanced nervously towards the stile. There was no one there. Realizing that his own figure would be visible in silhouette against the caravan's light grey paintwork, he hurried away in the shortest line to the edge of the field.

He stood in the shelter of the corrugated steel fence and kept watch for arrivals by way of the stile. It was not a comfortable vigil. A rising mist soon drove off the lingering warmth of the day. The air became damp and the chill of the soggy ground crept up his legs. Bats, hurling themselves in zig-zag quests, passed within inches of his face. An occasional moth made soft whirring contact with his skin. When this happened, he would shake himself frantically at the dusty, legged and whiskery, feathery, flailing creature that he imagined to be aiming for his mouth and nostrils. In the intervals between assaults by bats and moths, he listened apprehensively to rustling noises in the grass around him and fancied that he heard the gnashing of tiny, ankle-seeking teeth. Leaper was no nature lover.

He had almost made up his mind that he was paying too high a price for an uncertain and risky measure of libidinous entertainment when he caught the sound of approaching footsteps.

There was something odd about them. They came from somewhere nearer than the path beyond the stile, yet they rang upon a hard surface.

Leaper listened, puzzled and with increasing unease, as the firm unhurried footfall grew louder. Then suddenly there was silence. He stood tense and open-mouthed with the effort of estimating where his danger – and he felt sure it was danger – would reveal itself.

Several seconds passed. Leaper started: tiny metallic sounds had reached him, a scraping and a click. Behind him, were they? But. . . .

He threw himself flat at almost the exact moment when a section of the fence, a couple of yards from where he had been standing, swung out with a clangorous shudder.

Leaper kept absolutely still, his face pressed into a clump of wet and malodorous weed. Not until he had heard the gate replaced and locked and the swishing of feet through the grass die away did he turn his head and look towards the caravan.

A tall figure was standing there, to disappear a moment later into the black rectangle of the opening door. Bright light sprang from the windows and laid a glistening trail across the dew-beaded grass.

Slowly, Leaper rose to his feet, but kept close to the fence. The woman, he supposed, would be arriving very soon. He would have to wait until she, too, was safely behind the door and the curtains drawn before he ventured out of cover. Of course, she might not be coming. He would give her half an hour. It would be exceedingly awkward if he were to meet her on the narrow path back to the road.

A shadow crossed one of the windows. Leaper looked away from the light and tightly shut his eyes to restore their sensitivity to the night scene. On re-opening them he peered over to his left, trying to discern the outline of the group of trees beneath which was the stile. It was almost oppressively quiet now; even the moths seemed. . . .

The trees! They were there, blindingly clear. The fence, the field, the bushes, all flashed starkly upon his vision in an instant of electric-blue revelation. Then, in the scarlet-shot darkness that immediately followed, Leaper felt himself heaved and battered by a great bolt of noise.

His head feeling like a belfry tweaked by an earthquake, he reeled back against the fence. For some time he could see nothing; then gradually he became aware of a faint and irregular orange radiance where the caravan's windows had shone before. Unsteadily he walked out across the field.

As he drew near the caravan, the shape of what remained standing was thrown into relief by fire that crept among the wreckage within like glowing maggots. At least half the structure had been split away, leaving a skewed, open-fronted shed. While still twenty yards off, Leaper found himself stumbling over splintered spars and buckled panels.

The flames gained hold and brightened. He halted and looked about at what they revealed. A broken chair lay in a patch of nettles. Humped nearby was a small mattress. Flock had spilled from a rent in its cover and was being blown gently across the grass. The stove, lying on its side, was entangled in a tattered blanket.

The last thing Leaper saw before he turned and fled, retching, was the body almost under his feet.

It was understandable that he had not noticed it immediately for it had landed in a compact bundle within a slight hollow. Indeed, Leaper only recognized it for what it was when he bent down and saw the glint of a pair of shoes.

He prayed, as he ran, that he would not tread upon what his hasty, fearful examination had failed to account for . . . the body's arms and head.

11

"WILL YOU BE TAKING OVER THE ARRANGEMENTS for the inquest, sir?"

Sergeant Worple looked hopefully at Purbright, who had won his considerable respect by showing an interest in his envelope collection.

Purbright shook his head. "Oh, no, sergeant. That's decidedly Mr Larch's province. I'm not sure that I can claim to have anything more to do with the case now." He did not mention the telephone conversation with Hessledine half an hour previously when he had been strictly enjoined to 'get to the bottom of how that lunatic got the stuff to blow himself up with'.

"You will wait for the inquest, though, won't you, sir?"

"I wouldn't miss it for anything. Our inquests are absolute nightmares under old Amblesby; I want to know what a decently conducted one is like."

"Mr Chalice is an able gentleman and very sensible."

"There's no question as to what the verdict will be, I suppose?"

Worple pursed his lips. "No, not really, sir. It's just what everyone seemed to be expecting. He was a bit of a card, you know, this Mr Biggadyke. Had a name for getting up to queer tricks. Mind you: I must say I'm a tiny bit surprised, myself."

Purbright looked at him searchingly.

"Yes, sir. It's only a few days ago that I was sitting in with the chief inspector when he was questioning Biggadyke. Very much to the point, the chief was. As good as asked him straight out for an alibi. And Biggadyke told him about being over in Flax every Tuesday night."

"But you had only his word for that."

"Oh, I don't mean I believed in the alibi, sir. That sounded more like a tale for the wife than for the police. It's just that Biggadyke didn't strike me as the type. Bombs are tricky. They take intelligence."

"And this man wasn't especially intelligent?"

"Well . . . clever, yes" – Worple frowned and tugged his ear lobe – "but not up to anything really high-class. If you're with me, sir," he added doubtfully.

"I see what you mean," Purbright assured him. "But that isn't inconsistent with what happened. After three hits his cleverness ran out. He boobed. In any case it would be pushing coincidence rather far to suggest that in a town this size there are two characters mucking about with explosives."

"I expect you're right, sir. The chief has the same idea. Maybe that's why I was a bit doubtful."

Purbright made no comment. He was looking again at Worple's little stack of envelopes. "Didn't you pick anything up at the caravan?" he asked.

"Bits like those you mean, sir?"

"Yes. It must have been in the caravan that he made the things. Mr Larch said there was no trace of anything of the kind at his home or his office."

"That's right: it was me who went round to look. But I couldn't find anything where the caravan had been either. Of course, it was burned right out by the time the chaps in the lorry depot saw the fire and came round by the road and the path. Only Biggadyke had a key to that back gate."

Purbright put the envelopes back on the cupboard shelf. "You'd better not get rid of them yet awhile." he said.

Worple looked shocked. "Certainly not, sir. They're the only real evidence we've got."

Two days later Purbright was able to satisfy his curiosity as to what a 'decently conducted' inquest was like. He was favourably impressed, in particular by the grave but kindly efficiency of Mr Ben Chalice, the Chalmsbury coroner.

The almost total baldness of Mr Chalice lent disturbing emphasis to eyebrows that were like great bundles of wire. He had the long face of an habitual and careful listener. He never interrupted his witnesses, all of whom he treated with equal respect and patience, yet he had only to bring his penetrating gaze to bear upon the over-voluble or the pompous for them to stutter to a stop. He refrained from expressing any personal opinion, would not dream of impugning the character or intelligence of a witness, and had not been known in all the thirty-two years of his office to deliver a single platitude or homily.

It was hard to believe that Mr Chalice was a coroner at all.

The inquiry was held in the magistrates' court but with none of the ceremony to which the room might have lent itself. Ignoring the row of leather-backed chairs on the bench, Mr Chalice sat at the humbler level of the clerk's table. The four people who had been called to give evidence had found themselves places, at the coroner's invitation, around the same table. The scene would have resembled the meeting of a small firm's board of directors had it not been for the gaunt, overbearing presence of Larch, who stood behind the coroner's shoulder and looked mistrustfully at each of the assembly in turn.

Mr Kebble was wedged in the press box with three representatives of national newspapers who had been sent to extract what drama they could from the winding up of the affairs of the 'Tuesday Terror'.

Evidence of identification was given by the widow. She was a short, puffy-featured woman, the cream of whose former prettiness had long since been curdled by the demands and deviations of jolly Stan. Purbright watched from the back of the courtroom while Mrs Biggadyke, looking petulant rather than grieved, acknowledged that the body she had been shown in the Chalmsbury mortuary was indeed that of her husband, Stanley Porteous Biggadyke, a company director, whom she had last seen. . . . No, Purbright decided, she wasn't exactly devastated: the loss was to board rather than bed. It must have been a nasty moment in the morgue though. Had she guessed why Worple had kept one hand on the top of her husband's head while carefully slipping the sheet down a few inches?

"Do you know," the coroner was asking her gently, "if Mr Biggadyke was interested in explosives? Had he experimented with such things at any time?"

She gave a slight shake of the head. "He never told me anything about his outside interests. He spent quite a bit of time in the workshop at the firm. Or so he said."

"And in his caravan behind the depot?"

"He used that as an office. I never saw inside it."

Mr Chalice's steel-nibbed pen recorded her replies in flowing, generously looped script. It looked a slow business but Purbright found it soothing.

"Now I am going to mention three dates to you, Mrs Biggadyke, and I should like you to tell me, if you can, where you knew or believed your husband to be on those occasions. They are the nights of June the third, the seventeenth and the twenty-fourth. All were Tuesday nights."

She answered immediately. "He went to Flaxborough every Tuesday and stayed overnight. Every week it was, so I don't have to think of any dates."

"For what purpose did he go to Flaxborough?"

"It was what he called his club night. The Trade and Haulage Club. He didn't like driving home late, so he had an arrangement with a friend there to put him up for the night. Mr Smiles he was called. I never met him personally."

The coroner paused after writing this down. Then he said: "I think it is only fair to tell you at this stage that evidence will be given by Mr Smiles that your husband did not stay at his home on any occasion during the past three months. Would you care to say anything about that, Mrs Biggadyke?"

"Only that I'm not in the least surprised."

"I take it you did not enjoy your husband's confidence in all respects?"

"In no respect whatever." She spoke as if stating an obvious and not very important fact.

"I see. There is just one more point, I think, Mrs Biggadyke. From the series of Tuesdays I mentioned a short time ago one was missing. Tuesday, June the tenth. Can you say, of your own knowledge, where your husband was that night?"

The woman looked doubtful. "The tenth . . . no, well we've agreed I was wrong about him going where he said. To Flaxborough, I mean. So. . . ." Remembrance suddenly came to her. "Of course – that night I do know where he was. In hospital after his accident. He didn't come out until the Friday."

The coroner having read Mrs Biggadyke's deposition over to her slowly and clearly, she signed it. She was then directed by Chief Inspector Larch, mutely gesturing like an impatient head waiter, to remove herself a little further off. Her place next to the coroner was taken by the pathologist who had performed the post mortem.

The doctor's evidence confirmed that death had been due to severe multiple injuries, including decapitation, consistent with the victim's having been within short range of an explosion of considerable force.

"How short a range, doctor?" Mr Chalice asked.

"Oh, inches, I should say. There was a lot of burning on the front of the body. And, as I've said, the hands and forearms . . . well, they'd almost disappeared."

"Would you go so far as to say the deceased had probably been handling the explosive substance, whatever it was?"

"Certainly I should. I've no doubt in my own mind that that is what he was doing."

Again, at the instance of Larch, there was a shifting of places. The coroner found beside him a fat, sleek man in a brown suit. Mr Herbert Smiles wore that expression, half nervous, half challenging, of one who has made a lot of money just a shade too quickly. When he answered Mr Chalice's questions he spoke with throaty solemnity. One of the best, his tone proclaimed, had passed on, and you never knew but what you might be next yourself.

Had Mr Biggadyke been in the custom of visiting the Trade and Haulage Club at Flaxborough? Yes, he was a member and at one time had regularly spent an evening there each week.

And afterwards had he availed himself of Mr Smiles's hospitality until the following morning? He had, and very welcome had he been.

When had the custom lapsed? Oh, quite a while since — four months or more. They had met, yes, and had a few drinks from time to time. On good terms? Excellent terms, excellent. Yes.

"But in recent weeks, Mr Smiles, you are quite sure that Mr Biggadyke did not stay overnight at your house on Tuesday?"

"Not for several months, he hasn't. I'll be perfectly honest, mind — I did promise him I'd *say* that's where he'd been if anybody asked. But now the poor chap's passed on, well, I can only tell the truth."

"As you swore to do," the coroner dryly reminded him, nodding at the testament between them.

"Yes. As you say . . . of course." Mr Smiles regarded the little black book as apprehensively as if it had borne the imprint of the Commissioners of Inland Revenue.

The last witness was Sergeant Worple.

He presented, with a wealth of technical detail that Mr Chalice let pass without recording, an account of the demolition of the Courtney-Snell memorial, the beheading of Alderman Berry's statue, and the destruction of the great eye of Mr Hoole. No one, he observed, had been apprehended for the commission of these felonies (or crimes), which, at the time of the death of Mr Stanley Biggadyke were still officially ascribed to a person or persons unknown.

On the night of July the first, Sergeant Worple continued, a call was received at Fen Street police station from an officer of Chalmsbury Fire Brigade who reported the finding of a body near a burnt-out caravan at the rear of the premises of the Chalmsbury Carriage Company. He went to the scene that night and again the following morning. On the second occasion he was accompanied by Chief Inspector Larch and Constable Wraby.

Extensive inquiries were made and the site of the occurrence carefully examined.

The examination, though yielding clear indication that the caravan had been destroyed by an explosion and subsequent fire, provided no clues as to the cause of the explosion.

Inquiries also drew negative results apart from mutually corroborative statements by night drivers and fitters at the depot that the explosion occurred at 11.50 p.m. and was of considerable violence.

"These men knew, did they, that their employer had left the premises to go to his caravan?"

"Yes, sir. He arrived in his car at about 11.35 and told one of the mechanics to put the car in the garage. Then he walked down the yard to the fence and let himself through the gate into the field."

"Were you able to learn, sergeant, whether anyone other than Mr Biggadyke had access to his caravan?"

"I did ask that question of several of the staff, sir, and they all said he was the only person who ever used it. He kept it locked and no one else at the firm had a key to it – or a key to the gate in the back fence, for that matter."

"Did any of Mr Biggadyke's employees know for what purpose he used the caravan?"

"They had no certain knowledge, sir. One or two offered guesses but I did not encourage what seemed to me to be rather improper speculation."

The coroner glanced up at Worple, who was looking virtuous. "And that is all, is it, sergeant, that you can tell us? Nothing else occurs to you?"

Worple stared at Mr Chalice's pen for a few seconds then said suddenly and decisively: "No, sir."

The coroner leaned back, half turning, and addressed Larch. "Is there any question you would care to put, Chief Inspector?"

"I believe the witnesses have covered all the points that I can think of, sir."

Mr Chalice nodded and faced the table once more. Although he was sitting without a jury, he did not believe in recording a verdict without giving his reasons. He drew the grey hair tangles down over his bright, shrewd eyes and began to speak.

"As the last witness so properly remarked" – Worple's chin tightened with gratification – "guessing should not enter into an inquiry of this nature. Unfortunately, however, the evidence available to us is mainly of the kind that in a court of law would be called circumstantial. And forming conclusions from circumstantial evidence is a matter of putting two and two together: it is in some degree a speculative process. What we must guard against, of course, is making the answer more than four.

"Now, to start with, I am going to exclude the possibility that the four explosions of which we have heard today might have been unconnected incidents. The evidence leaves no doubt in my mind that the first three were contrived by one and the same person. What purpose that person entertained I cannot imagine, but some gesture or other would appear to have been intended.

"The fourth explosion did not follow the pattern established by the earlier ones. For one thing, it seems to have been the most violent of all. It was not staged in a public place, nor was it directed against a monument or symbol. An exhibitionist motive is not discernible.

"Moreover, it cost a human life.

"I conclude from these points of difference that the fourth explosion occurred spontaneously and accidentally.

"That brings us to its victim, Mr Stanley Biggadyke.

"It was his caravan in which the explosive substance lay – unless, of course, he had taken it with him when he left his car that night. In any case, he alone had access to the caravan, so we must presume that he was responsible for the explosive being there.

"That presumption is strengthened to virtual certainty when we take into consideration this fact. On all the nights when the first three explosions were engineered Mr Biggadyke had deliberately given a false account of his whereabouts and had even arranged for his story to be borne out by his friend, Mr Smiles, who today very rightly repudiated it.

"It is no part of my duty to accuse the deceased of

activities for which he might have been called to account in a court of justice. But in so far as those activities provide the only explanation of his death that seems tenable, I must express my view that Mr Biggadyke was the person responsible for the explosions on the third, seventeenth and twenty-fourth of June, and that he unintentionally caused the one which killed him in his caravan a week later.

"My verdict, accordingly, is death by misadventure."

"And no one," the man from the *Daily Sun* murmured to Mr Kebble, "could say fairer nor that."

12

MR KEBBLE COULD NOT REMEMBER WHEN LAST A policeman had bought him a drink. It was therefore with a feeling of pleasurable awe that he accepted the brandy that Inspector Purbright brought to their table in the Nelson and Emma.

"So it's all over, old chap," said Kebble, having plunged his brandy into a half tankard of water and pledged the inspector's health.

"It looks rather like it."

"You'll be going back now, I suppose. I'm sorry."

"That's nice of you, Mr Kebble. Actually, though, I shall probably hang on for a few more days. Chalmsbury's quite an attractive little town."

Kebble beamed, but about his eyes was a flicker of inquisitiveness. "What do you want, a list of the places of interest?"

"I have my own list, as a matter of fact. For what it's worth. I was wondering if you could give me a few directions, though."

"You don't want to bother Larch?" Kebble was still smiling.

"Well, I feel that would be somewhat ungracious of me. He's a busy man, is your chief inspector."

"Yes, isn't he?" Kebble sighed and took a slow drink. "All right, then; tell me where you want to go?"

Purbright revolved his glass on the smooth oak table top and eyed the dark, frothless column of beer. It was a sweet, oily local brew that soothed rather than stimulated. "For a start," he said, "I should like to take a trip into the past life of the gentleman on whose body Mr Chalice has just conducted his admirable inquest."

"So that's the sort of tour you're on, is it?" Kebble had started to clean his nails with a little pearl-handled penknife that hung from his watch-chain, and his voice seemed to come through the folds of his chin and neck.

"Idle curiosity," said Purbright. "This Biggadyke must have been quite a practical joker."

Kebble chuckled. "They tell me it was Stan who got in here one night after closing time and sawed all the handles off the beer pumps." He ruminatively surveyed the results of his manicure. "Then there was the beetle, of course. But you'll have heard about that."

"Beetle? No, I don't think so."

Kebble looked up. "Good lord! Haven't you really?" He brushed shut the little penknife across his palm. "I thought everyone knew about the Broadbeck beetle. Broadbeck – do you know where that is?"

Purbright shook his head.

"Never mind; it's a small village just outside the town. Biggadyke's house is there, next to the parish hall. The hall's a scruffy little place, but the rural district council has always used it for meetings and about three years ago they had an outside lavatory built – R.D.C. meetings are liable to go on all day, you know. Big was fearfully annoyed because they put the thing bang up to the edge of his garden, but there wasn't anything he could do about it.

"Of course the councillors were like kids with a new toy to begin with. Even after two or three months it still seemed to fascinate them. They kept popping in and out of council as if they didn't trust each other not to pinch the damn thing.

"It would be about the fourth monthly meeting after it was built that I could see something queer had happened.

The councillors were taking it in turn as usual to slope off when things got a bit dull and I happened to notice one of them come back looking pale and worried as hell. Then another tottered in a bit later in the same state. I kept an eye open after that and damn me if five or six didn't come back looking as if they'd seen a ghost.

"When the meeting was over, I thought they'd all get together and talk about whatever had happened outside. But they just shot off home without a word. Actually avoided one another. You'd have thought they'd just been tipped off that the bailiffs had called for the telly."

Kebble drank some of his brandy and water, glanced solicitously at the level of Purbright's beer, and went on: "I couldn't draw as much as a whisper for weeks afterwards. Then quite unexpectedly I got the whole story. It was the R.D.C. medical officer who told me.

"What put him on to it in the first place was the way one or two doctors in town pulled his leg. A bright lot you've got on that council of yours, they said to him. How do you mean, he said. Well, they said, half of 'em came rushing round to surgery the other night begging for confidential check-ups.

"The M.O. was tickled to death, naturally. He cornered one of the councillors he was fairly friendly with and wormed the truth out of him. The bloke admitted he'd thought something horrid was wrong with him because when he left the hall and began to pass water he got the most terrible burning and tingling sensation. He hadn't told anyone, except his doctor, because that wasn't the sort of thing he'd like spread around. He certainly didn't know that half the other fellows on the council had had exactly the same experience."

The editor paused to salute benevolently some new arrival in the tap room. Then he leaned further towards Purbright.

"Suppose," he said, "that you saw some insect or fly or something on the white porcelain of a urinal stall. Your natural instinct would be to try and flush it down, wouldn't it? I doubt if you or anyone else would be able to resist it. Well, what the M.O. found when next he was round at the village hall was a little beetle, oh, about that long"—he held up finger and thumb—"just where it would be most tempting." Kebble gazed admiringly into the middle distance. "He showed it to me; it was beautifully made."

"Copper?" ventured Purbright. "Soldered to a wire?"

Kebble seemed not to resent the expert short-circuiting of his tale. He smiled dreamily. "Aye, that's it. And a hole drilled right through, of course. They spotted the battery and the coil, or whatever it was, under Biggadyke's hedge." After a while he added: "Bloody good job he didn't use the mains, wasn't it?"

Purbright stared out of the window and watched the moving finger of a mast beyond the yard walls and outhouses. "Tide time," he murmured, obedient already to platitudinous custom.

"Aye," agreed Kebble. He shuffled off to the bar to buy more drinks.

When he returned the inspector invited him to give further details of Biggadyke's history, adding that he would accept the playful character of the man without more illustration.

Kebble obliged with the facility of one long drilled in obituary composition.

"Let's see, then," he began. "He was about forty-eight years old and a native of the town. He went to the Grammar School until he was asked to leave after some trouble with a girl. Big was always a pretty forward lad, which is odd in a way because he was absolutely hideous as a kid and didn't improve much as he got older. Never mind, he left school and went straight into his uncle's haulage business.

He played around for six or seven years, landed a few more girls into trouble, drank a lot of ale, joined the Rowing Club – you know the sort of thing. Then the old uncle crumbled: they tell me he took to writing backwards, you know. Anyway, he didn't last long after that and Big got the firm.

"He was no mug, mind. He knew the business by then and soon started to lay in the cash. Big had more sense than to pay for his wild oats out of capital; wine and women were for after office hours. In those days, at least; he relaxed a bit during the war when he was making more money than he knew what to do with. Of course, the business saved him from being called up.

"When did he get married, now? Oh, it must have been just after the war, 1946 maybe. His missus used to be one of the Jackson girls. Pretty, simpering little thing. I'll bet you didn't hear any girlish giggles from her today, though. She's spent the last ten years cooped up on her own in that whopping great ideal home exhibition out at Broadbeck. Big only used the place for sleeping, and not every night either."

"Any children?" Purbright asked.

The editor shook his head. Then he picked up his tankard and stared into it, tipping it slowly from side to side. "There's not much else I can tell you. As a matter of fact, the fellow was rather a dull number when you get down to a straight life story. We've quite a few of the same kind here. Not quite old enough to hoard their pennies and become respectable, but too old to play the fool without getting everybody's back up. You'd never believe the number of bald heads and pot bellies among that Rowing Club mob. One heave at an oar and they'd drop dead. It's all tankards and totty-tickling, old chap. Bloody desperate, if you ask me."

"Biggadyke wasn't in the Forces, you said. What about Home Guard or Civil Defence?"

"No, I think the Observer Corps was Big's war club."

"I'm just wondering where he might have acquired his taste for explosives."

"Can't imagine, old chap."

"Has that firm of his any connection with quarrying?"

Kebble looked doubtful. "I'd be surprised if it had. It handles agricultural stuff mostly. There's not a quarry within ten miles of here."

Purbright sighed. "You see my difficulty, don't you, Mr Kebble?"

"Oh, I do. Aye." The editor regarded him with a slightly too wide-eyed expression of sympathy. "You're trying to trace the . . ."

"Biggadyke's source. Exactly. Chalmsbury probably accepts these little diversions as perfectly normal, or at least in character. But what I must call the Authorities take a somewhat jaundiced view. High explosive, Mr Kebble, is the very apotheosis of un-Englishness. And when someone appears to have been in a position to stick free samples of it all over the place the Authorities are naturally concerned."

"I hadn't really thought of it like that," confessed Kebble. "Perhaps we do tend to be easy-going down here."

"Do you suppose Biggadyke might have known someone who would supply him with explosive? Or did he dream up all his practical jokes by himself?"

"He didn't know any safe-blowers, so far as I'm aware. Not that I'd rule it out."

"Had he any special friends?"

"Couldn't say. Wait a minute, though" – Kebble's eye had brightened – "male or female?"

"Either."

Kebble glanced about him, then beckoned Purbright to lean closer. "I'm going to tell you something, old chap, but for God's sake keep it to yourself." Again he looked quickly round the room. "That caravan was no more an office than this pub: you probably guessed that. Aye, but I bet you'll never guess who the totty was that old Big played gypsies with . . . Mrs Chief Inspector Hector bloody Larch, none other!"

He jerked back in his chair to enjoy the effect of his revelation.

At first, Purbright gave no sign of having heard. Then his lips slowly protruded in a soundless whistle. "Mr Kebble," he said at last, "this little township deserves to be administered by the Sodom and Gomorrah Joint Sewerage Board."

The editor nodded delightedly.

"You're not pulling my leg, are you?" Purbright was suddenly grave.

"Good heavens, no. Poor Leonard's too dumb to make up a story as good as that."

"Leonard?"

"The lad you've seen in the office. He's my reporter, or what I try and use for one."

"And what does he know about it?"

"He watched them together. It was very wicked of him and I fancy he feels rather guilty about it now, but I'm perfectly certain he was telling the truth. He even wrote what he called an 'exposure'." Kebble shuddered and reached for his drink.

"When did he see these . . . goings on?"

Kebble considered. "It was a Tuesday night: now which one? . . . Oh, yes – when old Barry Hoole's eye was blown out. I remember the boy saying that he heard the bang when he was just coming away from . . . Good Lord!" He stared at Purbright. "Then Big must have been in his caravan when the thing went off."

"Why not? He didn't need to be there with a match, you know."

Kebble subsided. "No, I suppose it had a time fuse or something."

"They all did. The first three, anyway."

"Aye, of course. Still, it does seem a bit odd to set a bomb ticking and then push off to a date with your totty. Damn me, I'd want to stay and see the fun if it was mine."

"Do you know Mrs Larch?"

"Not terribly well. She's Ozzy Pointer's girl, you know. Quite a good-looking lass but hard boiled. You'll not get much out of her."

"I shouldn't imagine her husband would thank me for trying."

"No. Quite so." Kebble looked at him shrewdly. "You might fare better with the old man, though. Ozzy's an awkward bloke but dead straight. He and his son-in-law don't hit it off too well, they tell me."

"Do you think Larch would have known of his wife's relationship with Biggadyke?"

"God, no! That's why I told young Leaper to be careful. If Larch did find out he'd go up to Hilda, give her a nice smile, and then slowly pull her head off like a prawn's."

"Hasty tempered, is he?"

"Not hasty, old chap. That wouldn't be so bad. He's the sort that wouldn't fall out with you until he'd got a grave dug ready. You want to watch your step with brother Larch."

Purbright promised that he would indeed.

"Now then," said Kebble, more cheerfully, "how's Mrs Crispin looking after you?"

"She's very" – Purbright groped for a word – "conscientious."

"Grand. I thought you'd be all right there. You're on your own except for old Payne, aren't you? Not that he'd bother you."

"On the contrary; we get along rather nicely. An ally is always welcome."

"What, against Mrs Crispin?" Purbright thought Kebble sounded slightly offended.

"No, no; but all lodgings are intimidating, however hard a landlady tries to make one feel at home. In fact it is precisely their homeliness that always alarms me. I half expect to find an embalmed mother propped opposite the teapot"

"Payne's been in digs for years," Kebble said. "He must be an authority."

"Oh, he copes expertly. But even the most competent, self-possessed lodger is essentially a sad fellow. And Payne is too intelligent to be able to hide it."

"You've spotted that? I'm glad. Sometimes I forget what I think of people – d'you know that? It sounds queer, but life drags on from year to year in a little place like this without anything happening to confirm an opinion. I mean nobody's going to give Payne or Barry Hoole a Nobel Prize, for instance, yet there was a time when they seemed absolutely brilliant."

"Talking of Hoole," Purbright said, anxious lest Kebble's sudden lapse into subjective philosophy should prove intractable, "I cannot fathom why he qualified for one of Biggadyke's infernal machines."

The editor brightened at once. "Oh didn't you hear the story?"

He might have known, Purbright reflected, that there would be a story. "No," he said, "I haven't heard that one either."

Kebble told him at some length about the sight testing, the belladonna, the collision.

"Rather a murderous trick," commented Purbright, a fraction more censoriously than he had intended. The editor looked surprised, then pained.

"Well, rather ill-advised, shall we say?"

Kebble accepted the amendment with a shrug. "Mind you," he said anxiously, "I only told you for your own amusement. Barry would be very upset if he thought that I'd let a confidence slip into the police files."

"It doesn't seem terribly important now that the man's dead. I shouldn't worry about it, Mr Kebble."

Kebble nodded gratefully. "Trouble is, old chap, we're used to the gendarmerie here being a bit on the heavy-handed side. They don't enjoy it, but Larch pushes them, you know. I can't get used to a policeman who isn't for ever holding a cell door open, as you might say."

"I don't want to spoil my holiday, that's all," Purbright said. "Let's go out and get sunburned, shall we? Then perhaps you can show me where Mr Pointer might be found."

13

AS IT HAPPENED, THERE WAS NO NEED TO SEEK OUT
Councillor Pointer. When Purbright and Kebble rose from
their table they saw him framed in the narrow, raised doorway, peering about him like an angry little sea captain
disturbed by voices in the hold.

Spotting them, he nodded curtly. "They told me I'd find
you in here."

Purbright marvelled once again at the omniscient 'they'
without whom, it seemed, all channels of information in
Chalmsbury would dry up. To Pointer he said: "Won't you
stay and have a drink, sir?"

The courtesy elicited only a sharp stare and "Aren't you
on duty?"

"Not rigidly so, sir. No."

Pointer grunted. "I never drink outside my own place
and even there it's only in the way of business. Doesn't do,
you know," he explained in a slightly more conciliatory
tone. He turned and led the way to the street.

In the sunshine Purbright was able to gain a clearer
impression of Larch's father-in-law. He saw a short, angrily
energetic man, whose restless and inflamed eyes had a faint
smile about them even when he was being offensive. His
moustache, though diminutive, was eloquent: it could
bristle furiously, twitch to an angle expressive of sceptical
amusement, or, most rarely, lie straight and sad in the
shadow of the councillor's cavernous nostrils and testify to
its master's essential simplicity.

"I'd like a word with you, Mr er . . ." – Purbright supplied his name and rank – "if you've time. You are the chap the Chief Constable sent over, I suppose? Oh, you needn't look coy, man. I know all about it."

Kebble, of whom Pointer seemed inclined to take no notice at all, decided that he was not going to be invited to share whatever frankness the wine merchant had in mind. He glanced at an imaginary sky-clock, appeared to note that it was much later than he had thought, said "Ah well," and strode off cheerfully.

Pointer led Purbright to his car, a large and costly pale blue affair. "I don't suppose," he said, "that you want to sit in a stuffy office on a day like this. We'll just have a ride round." He climbed in stiffly, stretched what he had in the way of neck until he could just see between the spokes of the steering wheel, and switched on the engine.

They left the town by the coast road, passed swiftly through the flat, intensively cultivated acres from which Chalmsbury drew most of its prosperity, and began to climb the gentle incline of the spine of hills on the town's eastern side.

Pointer kept silent save for an occasional terse comment on some feature of the landscape. He drew his companion's attention to several churches of a massiveness at odds with the obvious sparsity of population in these sleepy folds of pasture, trimmed with dark, narrow woods; and urged him once or twice to look back at a view of the receding plain, its patchwork of fields now obscured by the blue-grey haze of noon.

After about half an hour, Pointer slowed and drew the car on to a patch of turf on the brow of a hill more steep and rugged than the rest. Below them was the great scoop of a sandstone quarry. Behind lay the falling undulations of fields and woodland, ribboned with the yellowish lanes that linked hidden hamlets.

Almost immediately the car came to rest, it filled with the

oppressive scents of hot leather, rubber and steel. Purbright stepped out gratefully upon the short, springy grass.

"They say you can see both Chalmsbury steeple and Flaxborough Cathedral from here," Pointer informed him. They tested the theory but could discern neither. "Perhaps they mean with a telescope," added Pointer, sourly. "Still, it's as good a spot as any for a private chat. And I mean private, mind."

Purbright met his sharp, challenging stare with his own mild gaze. "You've no need to say anything at all if you don't wish to, sir. I've not sought this interview and I think you ought to remember that I'm not a private confidant, even if I have no official status here as a policeman."

Pointer shrugged and looked down at a handful of change he had taken from his pocket. "You're perfectly right, of course, Inspector. I realize I can't impose conditions on you : that was silly of me. The fact is that I'm rather worried."

"About the Biggadyke case, sir?"

"That comes into it, yes." Pointer cupped his hand and gently rattled the coins.

"But the affair's closed now. You don't disagree with the verdict, do you?"

"No, certainly not. It was what everyone expected. We went as near as we decently could – the council deputation, I mean – to telling the Chief Constable that Biggadyke was the fellow he ought to be after."

"The fellow your son-in-law ought to be after."

Pointer accepted the correction with a scowl. "Don't you worry : I'd already made sure that Hector knew the risk he'd be running if he ignored Stan Biggadyke, for all he was a personal friend – because of that, in fact."

"And he acted on your advice?"

"He certainly questioned Biggadyke officially. And with a witness. I don't think that any stories – malicious stories, mark you – about protection or turning a blind eye would stand up after that."

"A timely demonstration, was it, Mr Pointer?" Purbright's tone was guileless.

"If you like to put it that way. I'm quite sure that Hector was doing his duty without prejudice."

"Prejudice occasioned by friendship?"

"Yes."

"Tell me, Mr Pointer: did you approve of that friendship?"

Pointer answered without hesitation. "No, I did not. Biggadyke was a scoundrel. He was the last man in the town anyone in my son-in-law's position should have mixed with."

Purbright said nothing. His companion regarded the coins that he still shuffled irritably in his hand and finally thrust them back in his pocket. "Look here," he said, "what exactly did you come over here to find out?"

"Oh, come now, sir . . ."

"No, don't dodge, man. You weren't sent to help a bunch of country bobbies catch a joker who couldn't even work his own tricks properly. I'm not fool enough to believe that."

"What do you believe?"

"I'm not sure. Unless it's politics – is that it?"

Purbright smiled.

"You might well smile, Inspector, but I wouldn't put it past that Special Branch lot, or whatever they're called, to believe the blatherings of that poor idiot Mulvaney. He confessed, you know."

"Yes, sir. There was something mentioned about a Mr Mulvaney."

"Don't let him hear you call him mister. It's lieutenant. He thinks he's in the I.R.A. We've all known him for years, though. The poor fellow wouldn't know a bomb from a baby's bottle."

The inspector seemed preoccupied with the prospect of the opposite hill.

"Do you mind telling me, sir, if your daughter was friendly with Mr Biggadyke?"

Pointer stiffened. "My daughter?"

"Yes, sir. Mrs Larch."

"Both Hector and Hilda saw a good deal of him, I believe."

Purbright turned to face him. "Did you know that Mrs Larch was seen, on one occasion at any rate, to visit Biggadyke's caravan on her own and late at night?"

Pointer's expression changed, but not as Purbright had expected. Instead of furious disbelief, it registered bitter resignation. He shook his head slowly. "No, I didn't know."

"Do you suppose Mr Larch may have been aware of it?"

"It's very difficult to say. Hector keeps his feelings to himself. Some people think he hasn't any, but they're wrong. When there's something on his mind it just smoulders away until he can do something positive about it."

"At all events, he gave no sign?"

"Oh, no. Not the slightest."

"I don't want to intrude into your family's private affairs, Mr Pointer, but if I could have a word with your daughter . . . perhaps on your introduction and in your presence, if you wish . . ."

Pointer frowned. "Talk to Hilda? But what about?"

"About Mr Biggadyke, for one thing."

"Do you mean to say you're prepared to come over into another's man's police division and start snooping into his family affairs just because you've heard some unsavoury gossip about his wife? Damn it all, man, I think it's high time you told me exactly what you *have* been sent here to ferret out!" Pointer looked as if he had just swallowed a heavy draught of his own port.

"Very well, sir," replied Purbright patiently, "I'll tell you.

We wish to find where Biggadyke obtained his fireworks. Also, if at all possible, the real reason for his using them."

He hesitated. "You see, sir, there are three disturbing things about this case – disturbing, that is, when considered in association. One is the disappearance from a Civil Defence store in Flaxborough of a quantity of explosive. The second is the fact that Mr Larch is an instructor who has access to that store. Thirdly, as you've told me yourself, Mr Larch was a close acquaintance of the man we now know to have been addicted to blowing things up."

"Are you saying that the theft of that explosive has been traced to my son-in-law?"

"Not at all. The Chief Constable believes that one of the instructors must have taken it because they have keys to the store, but he might be adopting too narrow a view. From what I know of the place, almost anyone of moderate initiative could lift what he liked if he waited for an opportunity. The point is, though, that this Biggadyke affair lays Larch open to ten times as much suspicion as could possibly have attached to him otherwise."

"But why on earth should he have wanted to pass the stuff to Biggadyke – even if he did steal it?"

"I've wondered a good deal about that, Mr Pointer. I suppose you can see how serious some of the possibilities are?"

Pointer gave no sign of seeing anything of the kind.

"Your son-in-law," Purbright went on, "is an expert in the handling of explosives. Biggadyke, to the best of our knowledge, was not. But he couldn't resist spectacular jokes. It is conceivable, you know, that he might have been encouraged to dabble in what he didn't understand in the hope that he'd make a fatal mistake. Long odds, perhaps, but they could have been shortened by a wrong instruction. Detonators, now . . . they're extremely tricky little things, I understand."

"But that would be a wicked thing to do," exclaimed Pointer. "Absolutely wicked. Hector would never have thought of anything so dreadful."

"Not even if he'd learned of his wife's relationship with his friend?"

"I'm certain he didn't know of that. Hilda gave no one the slightest excuse for suspecting."

"You suspected, though, Mr Pointer."

"I happen to be the girl's father. Naturally I . . ." He faltered.

"What about her mother? Did she know?"

"Her mother? Good God!"

Purbright saw the wrinkled flesh around the councillor's little eyes constrict suddenly with bitter contempt. The revelation of marital loathing shocked him, but he repeated his question. "Did Mrs Pointer know of her daughter's affair?"

"I've no idea," said Pointer sullenly. "She . . . she doesn't discuss things with me."

Purbright waited. Pointer's earlier air of officiousness had gone. He seemed depressed and nervous. When finally he spoke, the edge to his voice was occasioned, Purbright thought, not by irritation but by fear.

"There's something I wanted to tell you before we got on to this business about Hilda. It's something that happened a year ago, but I've been thinking it over and I can't help feeling it might have had some connection with . . . with what you've been hinting."

He paused and continued more resolutely.

"I'm not going to give you any details, but this is roughly how things went. Last summer – it was just about this time of year – a girl was knocked down and killed by a car in Watergate Street. It was Stan Biggadyke's car, a great powerful sports thing, and Biggadyke was pretty drunk. He was arrested and taken to the police station. Hector was there and he took charge. He sent the sergeant out to fetch a doctor he said Biggadyke had chosen to examine him. The doctor was out of town. There were some more delays and by the time a doctor did arrive Biggadyke was dead sober. A case went to the assizes but although the policeman who made the arrest stuck to his story that Biggadyke had been drunk at the time the fellow was acquitted. The lack of medical evidence and a good bull-shitting barrister saved him.

"What puzzled everyone who knew Biggadyke and his habits was how he'd managed to sober up so quickly in the cells. There were rumours of pep pills and cold douches and so on, but I knew that no drunk would have been able to get up to tricks like that while an experienced policeman was keeping an eye on him."

Pointer gave a short, mirthless laugh. "That's what I thought, anyway. Then about a couple of months after the trial I happened to be in the White Hind on business when I heard Biggadyke braying away just behind me at the bar. He was pretty far flown and I was just about to scoot out of range before the damn fellow spotted me. Then something he said caught my ear.

"I'll never forget it. 'Payne, old man', he said – he'd buttonholed that blackguard who lodges at your place – 'Payne, old man', he said – and these were his exact words – 'if ever you get pulled in for being drunk, just ask for a bucket of Larch's luscious larrup.' That's what he said. Payne asked him what he meant but I couldn't hear any more after that."

"You drew your own conclusions, though?"

"I did, Mr Purbright. And I think I was right, too. You see, I once asked Hilda whether she packed supper for Hector when he stayed late at the station. She said no, nothing to eat, because if he wanted it the caretaker's wife would make him a few sandwiches. But he often took a big flask of coffee, she said. Strong and black was how he liked it."

Pointer was silent. Then he looked with anxious appeal at Purbright. "You'll not take this any further, will you? I mean . . . well, nothing could be proved now, anyway."

"Why have you told me this, Mr Pointer?" Purbright asked quietly.

"It's worried me. That's one reason. I have public responsibilities and I've always liked to have a clean conscience. You've no idea what an ordeal it was for me when I was pushed on that deputation to the chief. I'd been told that people here suspected Hector of covering up for Biggadyke. But theirs were only suspicions. I knew damned well he'd protected him once before and got him off one of the most serious charges in the book."

"Can you suggest why, sir?"

"Does it matter?"

"It may matter a great deal."

Pointer shrugged. "Well, Hector owed Biggadyke money, for one thing. Quite a lot, I believe. And Biggadyke had helped him in other ways. Socially and so forth. He was generous enough to anyone he palled up with, I'll say that for him."

"I see. So you don't think it likely that Mr Larch could have wished him any harm? You reject that rather fanciful theory of mine about Biggadyke's accident?"

"That Hector kidded him on to play with explosives, you mean."

Purbright nodded and waited.

"No," said Pointer in a low voice, "I don't reject it, and that's the truth. Just now when I said that Hector wouldn't be capable of doing such a thing, it was because . . ."—he spread his hands in a gesture of helplessness—"Oh, I don't know: he's a member of my own family. But of course he's capable. It's just the sort of method he'd choose."

"And are you still convinced that Mr Larch never found out about his wife's meetings with Biggadyke?"

Purbright saw that Pointer was trembling. He sat down on the grass and motioned the wine merchant to join him.

Pointer squatted, wiping his brow and staring gloomily across the valley. "I know this much," he said. "If Hector does find out about Hilda – and it must be common knowledge when you managed to pick it up so soon – if that happens, I wouldn't give much for my girl's chances." Pointer clutched the policeman's arm. "Suppose she'd been with Biggadyke that night in the caravan. It could have been meant for her, too."

"Look, sir," said Purbright, "I think we'd be wise at the moment not to envisage too many possibilities. The chances are that your son-in-law is a perfectly decent and harmless fellow and that your daughter's in no danger whatever. They'll probably get over their troubles like any other married couple who hit a bad patch."

He hoped that these shameless platitudes would have sedative effect upon poor Pointer. The last thing he wanted was for the man to panic; he had underestimated his vulnerability to suggestion.

But Pointer showed an entirely unexpected reaction. Mottled with sudden anger, he stared savagely at Purbright. "What the hell do you think you are? A marriage counsellor?"

"I'm sorry; I don't quite. . . ."

"You don't quite," Pointer mimicked bitterly. "Oh, but you do quite. You must have got something for your rooting and grubbing. They'll have been ready enough to tell you."

Purbright watched the inflamed, protuberant little eyes. To his embarrassment, they were beginning to flood with tears of self-pity.

He shrugged gently. "Unless I know what you're talking about, sir. . . ."

"Lovers, Mr Purbright." He forced out the word like a

distraught shop girl pronouncing some indelicate medical term for the first time. "They run in families, you know. But of course you must know. A busy-bodying detective inspector. My God, man, they even told me! The very day I got back."

Purbright divined that he was expected to help the man play out some familiar rite of self-abasement. "I see," he murmured.

Down the wine merchant's memory-puckered cheek a tear rolled. "I was away in France all that fortnight. In the Rhone Valley. An extraordinary summer. Marvellous." He looked woodenly at Purbright. "But you'll remember it yourself, I expect?"

Purbright glanced warily at his watch. "Hadn't we better be getting back now, sir?"

"I asked you," said Pointer in the tone of a moneyed diner putting a waiter in his place, "if you remembered the summer we had in 1937."

The inspector gave a controlled sigh. "Not very clearly, sir. It . . . was a long time ago, wasn't it." He got up and stood by the car.

Pointer remained sitting in silence for a few seconds more, then rose and climbed in behind the wheel. When next he spoke it was to draw Purbright's attention to some village church.

14

MRS CRISPIN FULLY REALIZED THAT GENTLEMEN
boarders needed an adequate substitute for the ministra-
tions of absent or non-existent mothers and wives. They
were deprived creatures, leading an unnatural life from
the moment when they returned from business (she used
the term with flattering lack of distinction, whatever their
employment) until they retired to that good-night-sleep-
tight whither they were consigned some five hours later
by their guardian, still beamingly solicitous as she stood
holding ajar the door of the staircase cupboard and beginning silently to count up to the hundred at which she would
switch off the electricity and glide to her own chaste
and immensely strong couch in the kitchen.

But how could the gentlemen's exile from homes proper
and complete be rendered less arid? She had given the
question much thought and it was in accordance with her
conclusions that the appointment, furnishing and tending
of the gentlemen's sitting room had evolved.

Cosiness, Mrs Crispin had mused, was what the
domestic male valued above all else. She therefore sank
some of her capital in a hook and staple whereby the door
connecting the sitting room and kitchen could be held open
on winter evenings, thus allowing air warmed by the
kitchen stove to circulate freely through both apartments.

Mrs Crispin considered next the frequent use, in
magazine stories about happily integrated husbands, of
such adjectives as *old*, *battered*, *well-thumbed*, *chewed*,
shapeless. These, she noticed approvingly, nearly always

appeared in conjunction with *favourite* (*his favourite old pipe/hat/old easy chair, moulded into comfortable contours by his grateful frame, etc.*) Such guidance to masculine predilections in the furnishing line was perfectly clear, and Mrs Crispin followed it faithfully.

She showed consideration for eyes tired after a day at business by making the room lighting as discreet and restful as a single forty-watt bulb could render it.

The same motive partly dictated her decision not to install a television set, but in this case, too, she was influenced by her gleaned knowledge of male psychology. In the comfort of their well-moulded old easy chairs, their favourite pipes drawing well, men wished to chew the fat and swap yarns, not to gaze dumbly at a little screen.

Unfortunately for Mrs Crispin's careful designs, neither Cornelius Payne nor Inspector Purbright shared her idealist conception of manly leisure. After the celebration of high tea, they would retreat, a trifle furtively, to one or other of their bedrooms and there play chess.

On the evening after Purbright's excursion with Councillor Pointer, it happened to be Payne's turn to provide hospitality. This meant that he sat on his bed while his guest occupied a small cane-seated chair by the window. The chess board was set between them on a pile of three suitcases.

Purbright was by far the inferior player and Payne had handicapped himself by a bishop, a rook and two pawns. His victory would thereby be postponed long enough for the game to last until dusk when Phyllis, prompted by a mistress who associated lodgers' silence with suicidal intentions and a possible sudden rise in the gas bill, would burst in and ask if they were ready for supper.

"How did the inquest go?" asked Payne, opening the game with one of his depleted pawns.

Purbright surveyed the board while he reached for

cigarettes. "Misadventure," he said. "All it could be really."

"Wouldn't an open verdict have suited?"

"Too vague. All right for drownings. Explosions, no."

"There couldn't have been much evidence, though." Payne accepted a cigarette and struck a match for them both.

"Nothing direct. It really boiled down to the rejection of coincidences. One, two, three explosions in a small town. Then another. How could they be dissociated? Then there was Biggadyke's reputation, of course." Purbright leaned forward and moved a pawn.

Payne placed a finger lightly on one of his knights and considered. "His reputation, yes. . . ." He moved the knight to threaten Purbright's advancing pawn. "But what evidence could be brought to prove reputation?"

"None, now that you mention it. It seemed taken for granted."

"Not very legal. Did no one suggest why he had been doing those curious things?"

"Motives weren't questioned. It might have been interesting if they had been."

Payne smiled. "You haven't been making guesses, then?"

"The coroner seemed to assume that the man was simply an exhibitionist. I never met him, but from what others have said about him I should think that explanation is the most logical, bald as it is. Did you know him, by the way?"

"Slightly."

Purbright catalogued. "Arrested development; pot-pinching sense of humour; technical expertize of sorts, combined with irresponsibility and a touch of dipsomania. How's that?"

"Not bad," Payne said. "Actually, though, there are thin threads of reason running through . this business, you know."

"Ah, now those," Purbright said promptly, "I should like to hear about." Spotting the threat to his pawn he moved out a knight to cover it. "Let's take the explosions in order. What grudge did he bear the drinking fountain?"

"Not an aesthetic one, I assure you, though God knows that would have been understandable. No, the thing was a memorial. It was put up by the widow of a man called Courtney-Snell. And Courtney-Snell, in his time, had won an action for slander against Biggadyke."

"Posthumous vengeance, you think?"

"Niggardly; but satisfying, perhaps."

"All right. And the statue?"

Payne paused to open a path for his remaining bishop. "The statue," he repeated. "That gesture was a little less personal, but if you knew Chalmsbury you would appreciate it. Does the name of the late Alderman Berry mean anything to you?"

Purbright shook his head.

"He was a notable zealot – or notorious bigot – according to taste," Payne said. "I scarcely remember him, but they say that when he died the local brewery issued their draymen with white ribbons to wear in their hats."

"A warrior of abstinence."

"He was indeed. He also made a great deal of money, with a modest fraction of which he endowed an ugly chapel, so canonization – in Chalmsbury terms – was inevitable. We immortalized him in gunmetal, or whatever it was that Biggadyke found so challenging."

"You suggest, then," said Purbright, bringing up another pawn, "that Biggadyke's second onslaught was that of a drinking man upon a totem of teetotalism."

"You express it neatly. Yes, a gesture of principle, I should say. Biggadyke was not richly endowed with principles, so he was all the more likely to proclaim spectacularly what few he had. Had he lived, I feel he might have founded a Fellowship of Bad Templars."

Purbright silently scrutinized the new position of Payne's queen, which his opponent had just moved to the van of his bishop. Then he said: "And what of the great eye of Mr Hoole? That affair has a Kiplingesque flavour, to my mind."

"The most intriguing of the three," Payne agreed. He groped beneath the bed and produced a bottle. Without taking his eyes from the board, Purbright felt in his pocket and handed Payne a corkscrew. Soon they were sipping from tooth glasses one of Councillor Pointer's more moderately priced clarets.

"You've met Barrington Hoole, I presume," said Payne.

"Fleetingly, yes."

"Quite a brilliant chap, oddly enough. We were in the same year at Cambridge. I never dreamed then that we'd wind up by being fellow shopkeepers. However. . . ." Payne eyed his wine quizzically and scratched a fragment of dried toothpaste from the glass rim with his nail. "It seems he was rather unkind to the oaf Biggadyke — absolutely deservedly – about a month ago. Hence, I think, the reprisal on the eye. He was very fond of it, poor chap," Payne added sadly.

Purbright blocked with a pawn the line of threatened advance by Payne's queen, and went on: "The question that no one seems able to settle is where Biggadyke obtained his explosive. It looks as though I shall have to go back without an answer."

Payne looked up. "So that's why they sent you, is it? I was wondering if you were M.I.5 or something. Kebble's convinced of it."

Purbright grinned. "That's probably because I took your advice and was shockingly indiscreet. Tell me, though, from what you know of Biggadyke how do you imagine

143

he'd set about that queer campaign of his? Where would he get the stuff?"

Payne considered. "As a haulage contractor he made some useful, if questionable, contacts during the war, I believe. Perhaps there's a black market in gelignite, or something."

"There is, unquestionably. But I should suppose that quotas are pretty well taken up by gentlemen with banking interests. I'd be most surprised to learn that Mr Biggadyke had been able to whistle any his way. Anything else occur to you?"

Payne poured out some more wine before replying. "There was a rumour," he said slowly, "of some explosive having disappeared from that Home Guard place. . . ."

"Civil Defence," Purbright corrected.

"Yes, but that's at Flaxborough anyway. You'll know all about it."

"Not all, no. But the connection with this lot seems very tenuous."

Purbright returned his attention to the game. Payne's last move, he noticed, appeared to have no immediate object. But his own interest had waned and he contented himself with advancing another pawn. After quite a long silence he asked: "Would it be possible, do you think, for Biggadyke to have manufactured his explosive himself?"

Payne hesitated. "Chemically, you mean?"

"Yes. Say it were some nitro compound. Nitro . . . well, nitro-glycerin: I suppose that's the best known."

Payne thoughtfully caressed the waxed points of his moustache, then shrugged. "Feasible, I imagine. Very dangerous, though." He got up and crossed the room to a bookcase. "There may be something among these that will help. They're a little out of date as textbooks go but organic chemistry is less subject to fashion than physics."

Purbright watched him kneel and pull out, one by one,

the books on the bottom shelf. The lettering on the spines of most of them was nearly indiscernible; they probably had been second-hand when Payne acquired them in his university days.

At last Payne found the volume he had been seeking. He reached up and put it on the top of the case between a pair of photographs while he tidied the rest of the row. Purbright glanced idly at the two pictures. One was a faded sepia portrait of a woman in late Victorian or Edwardian dress; the other was of a small girl standing beside a television camera.

Payne brought the book over, referred to its index and thumbed back to the section he wanted.

"Simple enough in theory," he said after a while. "Allow a mixture of concentrated nitric and sulphuric acids to act on ordinary glycerin and separate the oily liquid that rises. There you have it – nitro-glycerin."

"Well, then: even Biggadyke. . . ."

Payne shook his head. "No, I said it was simple in theory. But the stuff is deperately unstable, remember. You can't carry it around like lemonade. One good jolt and – whoosh!"

"Yet dynamite is safe enough to handle, surely. Isn't that nitro-glycerin in some form or other?"

Payne turned a page. "It is, actually. Hang on a minute." He read further through the text. "Yes, here we are: they absorb the liquid nitro-glycerin in something called kieselguhr."

"And what's that?"

"No idea. Here it just calls it 'an inert, clay-like substance'."

Purbright, feeling somewhat inert himself, said nothing for a few moments. Payne closed the book and waited.

"Detonators," Purbright said suddenly. "All these time-bomb things are set off by detonators, aren't they?"

"Yes, I suppose they are." Payne frowned at the cover of the textbook. "I don't think this would be any use," he said. "You're still thinking along do-it-yourself lines, are you?"

"More or less."

"Well, the only detonating agent I can call to mind is mercury fulminate. I don't know whether it's still used nowadays."

"It could be made at home, though? Or something like it?"

"I wouldn't like to say offhand."

Purbright stretched, yawning. "Never mind," he said, "it all sounds terribly unlikely. Anyway, from what I've heard of Biggadyke I can't picture him tackling anything so complicated."

Payne smiled gently and began to pour more wine. "We all have our unsuspected talents," he observed.

The next morning, Purbright caught an early train to Flaxborough in order to report upon his perplexities to the county chief constable.

Mr Hessledine's manner was courteous but clinical. He had, he said, studied already a verbatim report of the inquest. The affair had been closed to the coroner's satisfaction, certainly, but the essential question of the source of that impossible fellow's explosive had not even been touched upon. One of his officers was under a cloud, and he trusted that Mr Purbright had produced evidence sufficient either to eliminate Chief Inspector Larch – which was much to be desired – or to prove his complicity. Now then, what had Mr Purbright to say?

Mr Purbright confessed unhappily that he was in no position to relieve the Chief Constable of his doubts one way or the other. He had been unable to resolve the ominous coincidence of the explosions and the theft from the Civil Defence store. Worse, far worse, his inquiries had revealed a relationship between Biggadyke and the chief inspector that was at once paradoxical and pregnant with possibilities that did not exclude murder itself.

Hessledine listened impassively to the account of Larch's friendship with Biggadyke; of the local rumours of their collusion; and of the seduction of Hilda Larch.

When he had finished, he looked apologetically at the Chief Constable and said: "I don't seem to have made matters any easier, do I, sir?"

Hassledine gave him a magnanimous smile. "You've been very thorough, Mr Purbright. I'm only sorry that you found yourself placed in such invidious circumstances. Of course, I had no idea that. . . ." He blinked and left the sentence unfinished.

"Quite so, sir."

Hessledine rose from his desk and walked gracefully to the window. "The proper thing to do now," he said to his reflection in its panes, "would be to suspend Mr Larch from duty until some sort of an official inquiry could be made. But you see the difficulty, don't you?" He half turned in Purbright's direction.

"I think I do, sir. You mean that if nothing more definite could be established, Mr Larch would appear to have been unjustly treated."

"Exactly. Tantamount to wrongful arrest." The Chief Constable shuddered and faced the window again. "I wonder," he said very quietly, "if Mrs Larch could be prevailed upon to help."

"I really don't know, sir; I haven't yet met Mrs Larch."

"You don't fancy trying?"

"No, sir."

"Ah." Hessledine nodded thoughtfully. "It would be rather awkward, wouldn't it? Snooping on the wife of a colleague. I wouldn't ask anyone to do that. Not unless some serious crime were involved. On the other hand, it is sometimes possible to have a confidential chat without giving offence or sowing suspicion, you know."

Purbright said nothing.

"Of course," the Chief Constable went on smoothly, "if you do happen to meet Mrs Larch in propitious circumstances at any time, I'm sure you won't allow false chivalry to blind you to her possible value as a witness." He waved his hand elegantly. "After all, she must have been moderately fond of this Biggadyke person. She ought to have some idea of what he was up to, if anyone has. And for all we know she might be eager to tell."

"There's just one thing I should like to know, sir."

"Yes?"

"Has it occurred to anyone to ask Chief Inspector Larch about this explosive that is supposed to be missing?"

Hessledine moved a little from the window and stared at him. "I don't think you quite understand," he said. "Discrepancies in Civil Defence stores are a most serious matter. National security is involved." He paused to make sure Purbright was impressed.

"Strictly between ourselves," he went on, "this matter came to light as the result of stocktaking. No one apart from the Civil Defence Officer and the county committee has been told. They asked me to make confidential inquiries. It so happens that you've been, well, unlucky so far; but, my goodness, Mr Purbright, I do hope you realize the whole thing is fearfully hush-hush."

He leaned forward from the waist to emphasize the import of his final sentence: "It's quite on the cards that the Home Office will come into it."

"I take it, then, that Mr Larch has not been questioned, sir."

"Certainly not. The C.D. Officer was most insistent on maximum secrecy. He was in Intelligence during the last war you know. Very well up in this kind of thing."

"I still think you should tackle Mr Larch directly, sir."

The Chief Constable raised his brows. "Aren't you being a little direct yourself, Mr Purbright?"

"You might put it that way, sir."

There was a short silence, during which Hessledine seemed to find his left cuff-link a new and intriguing subject of study.

"You feel you would rather not proceed with this investigation: is that so?"

"Not in the role of a sort of security policeman. It goes very much against the grain."

The faintest flush appeared in Hessledine's cheek. "Just as you like, Mr Purbright. I should be the last to expect you to undertake anything you felt to be unethical." He paused. "If I can think how Larch might be approached tactfully I may have a word with him. Meanwhile you'd better stay on in Chalmsbury for a couple more days just to give the impression that you're clearing up the loose ends. I don't want coroners to get the idea that they've only to say the word for the police to go skipping off like hired ponies."

"Then you wish me to return to my own division at the end of the week, sir?"

"I think so, yes. I shall let your chief know, of course."

They parted with cool formality.

15

BARRINGTON HOOLE HUMMED CONTENTEDLY AS HE dangled his short, plump legs from the visitor's chair in the *Chronicle* office and read the galley proof of Kebble's account of the inquest.

"A fitting consummation," he remarked when he had finished.

Kebble rolled up the proof and put it like a telescope to his eye.

"Guess who saw it happen," he invited, squinting round the room.

"Saw what happen?"

"Stanley's catastrophe, old chap."

"I didn't," said Hoole. "Worse luck."

Kebble grinned and brought the paper tube to bear on Leaper, gloomily occupied with scissors and paste at his desk. "He did."

Hoole turned, then looked back at Kebble. "You're not being funny?"

The editor shook his head.

"Good Lord!" said Hoole, then, more softly: "But he didn't give evidence, did he?"

"He's told nobody but me. He was there all right, though. Nearly trod on the corpse."

"Shouldn't he have gone to the police?"

"What, and be third-degreed by Larch?"

Hoole wrinkled his nose. "You've a point there."

"All the same, the lad is going to talk to a policeman. I advised him to." Kebble had lowered his voice still further.

"You remember that Flaxborough fellow I mentioned? He's coming in this morning."

"The local force must be far gone in corruption if outsiders need to be imported to look into our fatalities. Anyway, I thought the whole thing had been cleared up at the inquest."

Kebble leaned close. "They tell me this Purbright's an absolute bloodhound. He must be on to something or he'd have left by now." He added that he had met the inspector and found him an uncommonly decent fellow.

"Obviously an imposter," propounded Hoole. "All policemen are repressed rapists. Tell me: Did you look at his neck?"

"Not specially. Why?"

"Their necks are characteristic. Bright pink. Hairless. Like columns of luncheon meat straight out of cans."

The street door swung open. "Here he is now," muttered Kebble. He got up and hurried round the counter.

Purbright allowed himself to be led to a chair at the back of the office, where Kebble presented Leaper to him in the manner of a farmer dubiously confronting a veterinary surgeon with an ailing sheep. The editor then returned to his conversation with Hoole, having first stolen a glance at Purbright's neck. "Not a bit like meat," he announced, resuming his seat. "Perfectly nice chap."

The inspector had little heart for his interview, which he had undertaken solely out of good nature. Yet as he listened, at first with politely concealed indifference, then with a sharpening sense of this youth's having unknowingly observed something significant, he realized that he was now more eager to discover the truth than at any time since his arrival in Chalmsbury.

"You say there was a hole in one of the caravan windows. Do you mean the window was smashed?"

"No, the rest of the glass was all right. There was just

this hole low down. Nearly round. No jagged edges."

"Was it light enough for you to see that?"

"Oh, yes. You'd be surprised how bright it is out in the open, even quite late." Leaper's tone indicated pity for the inspector's lack of experience.

"Would you say that the window was the kind that opens? You know, like a transome window, hinged at the top, that you can push outwards?"

"That's right. It was like that."

"So it would have been possible to put your hand through the hole in the glass, unfasten that little bar thing with holes along it, and pull the window open?"

Leaper scowled. "I didn't touch it."

"I know you didn't," said Purbright patiently. "I just want to know if anybody else could have done so."

"No reason why not."

"Right. Now you said something about a shelf, or fixed table."

"Just under the window, yes. There'd been bottles and things on it the first time. Not when I saw it again, though."

"What was on it the second time? Anything?"

"It looked like a box. I could only make out the shape. Like a shoe box."

"A parcel, do you think? In paper and string?"

The youth considered. "I didn't notice if it was wrapped up. The light wasn't all that good." He looked defensively at Purbright, who smiled and said never mind, he'd been remarkably observant and without doubt would be most successful in his chosen career.

"Oh, there's just one other thing, Mr Leaper" – for the second time in his life Leaper was warmed by a respectful form of address and he helpfully perked his head – "Did you happen to meet or see anyone on either of the nights when you went out to Mr Biggadyke's caravan? Apart from the lady, of course."

"I didn't see anyone the second time. Not as to remember."

"And the first time?"

'Kebble's boy' hesitated for only a moment before replying: "I did meet someone then. It must have been nearly midnight. I met Mr Hoole."

The subject of this confidence, Purbright noticed, was no longer in the office. Kebble, alone, was sharpening a pencil with slow deliberation. As each shaving fell he picked it from his waistcoat and dropped it into an ashtray. Purbright walked across and sat in the chair lately vacated by Hoole. Kebble grinned at him and shut the penknife with his perilous palm-sweeping action.

"Like some coffee?" The editor squeezed out of his seat and went to a door marked Ladies. "Put an extra cup on, ducky," he shouted at its handle.

Nearing his desk once more, he accepted one of Purbright's cigarettes. As he was lighting it, he made with his free hand a gesture of sudden recollection and smokily announced: "Something to show you, old chap; hang on." He bobbed down and Purbright heard a drawer open.

"This," said Kebble, handing him a sheet of paper on which was pasted a cutting, "went in last week's issue. What do you make of it?"

Purbright read the five lines of verse, then shrugged. "What's it supposed to be?"

"It's an 'In Memoriam'. At least, it was sent in as one. There was no name or address given but the money came with it so we printed it. I thought it was a bit odd; there seemed no harm in it, though." He paused and added: "Now I'm not so sure."

Purbright read the cutting again more slowly. He heard Kebble say: "Look at the date."

"July the first."

Kebble nodded. "The day Biggadyke blew himself up."

"Do you mean you think he sent this in himself? A suicide proclamation, as it were?"

"What, Stan? Poetry?" The editor's voice sounded like a skidding car.

"But you do suggest a connection?"

Kebble hitched his chair forward in a businesslike way and turned the paper sideways so that they both could read it. "I don't know if you ever look at these 'In Memoriam' things," he said, "but you can take it from me that this one's a bit out of the ordinary. For a start, it doesn't make sense – not that all the others do, for that matter, but at least people know what's meant by 'Sleep on, dear father' provided the bloody printer hasn't left the comma out, which has happened before now, incidentally. Then the number of lines is odd. Listen. . . ." He intoned, with exaggerated emphasis on metre:

"The thirst that from the soul doth rise
  Doth ask a drink di-vine.
  There'll be that dark pa-rade
  Of tassels and of coaches soon:
    It's easy as a sign. . . .

"Well – you see what I mean, old chap."

Purbright thought he did. "The thing's curiously disjointed, isn't it? But modern verse often is."

"Modern?" echoed Kebble. "Oh, no; it's not modern – not with a 'doth' in it."

"It's familiar, though, somehow." Purbright closed his eyes and murmured several times: 'The thirst that from the soul doth rise. . . .'"

"Hoole would know," said Kebble, watching the inspector's face. "I should have asked him just now. He's an expert on poetry."

"Something to do with school," Purbright said, his eyes still closed. "A song, surely. . . ."

154

His trance was broken by the arrival of Muriel. She placed on the desk the two brimming cups she had carried carefully and silently from the place of their concoction. Purbright sniffed and opened one eye. Then he sat suddenly upright. "Drink to me only!" he exclaimed.

Muriel glanced nervously at Kebble and departed.

Purbright pointed at the cutting. "That's it. *Drink to me only with thine eyes and I'll not ask for wine – The thirst that from the soul doth rise doth ask a drink divine*. The rest doesn't belong. It's from something else altogether. The final rhyme is fortuitous."

"Then why have the two been stuck together?" Kebble asked.

"We can come back to that. For the moment I think we might consider them separately. You don't happen to have any verse anthologies handy, do you?"

Kebble, suspecting irony, at first made no reply. Then he noticed that Purbright was looking at him expectantly. "I can send Leonard round to the library," he offered. "It's only in Fen Street."

Leaper, flattered by his being dispatched on so extraordinary an errand, returned within quarter of an hour bearing half a dozen volumes.

"We'll probably find the Ben Jonson in Palgrave," said Purbright in a manner so suggestive of familiarity with such things that Kebble stared quite rudely at him for several seconds.

"Yes, here we are." Purbright quickly scanned the whole poem. "There seems nothing significant in the rest of it. Now why were those two particular lines chosen? Thirst – a spiritual thirst. That might be longing, a regret for someone dead. It fits the context of an epitaph, anyway. A drink divine, though. . . . What would that represent, do you think?"

"Brandy," responded Kebble, without hesitation.

"It could be some sort of spiritualist cliche. Contact with the departed, you know." He shook his head. "No, they would incline more to abstentionist metaphor."

There was a pause.

"What about revenge, old chap?"

"I doubt if Ben Jonson was after quite that effect. Still, he doesn't really come into it. Vengeance it might be. That would tie with the second quotation, at any rate."

"The 'dark parade' bit?"

"Yes. You notice the future tense. Threatening, isn't it?"

Kebble looked again at the cutting, his lips moving. Suddenly he shut his eyes tightly and groaned. "Damn me if I havn't only just tumbled! A funeral!"

"Oh, yes," said Purbright with mild surprise. " 'Tassels and coaches' – an evocative phrase." He was about to close the book when something caught his attention. He looked up at Kebble. "Do you know anyone called Celia?"

"Celia . . . no, I don't think so. Why?"

"Well, everyone thinks of this poem – or the song, rather – as 'Drink to me only'. But its actual title is 'To Celia'." He picked up the cutting. "These things refer to anniversaries, don't they, as a rule?"

"Always. The genuine ones do, anyway," Kebble added grimly.

"Do you think that if you worked back through the files you might come across someone called Celia who died on the first of July?"

"Possibly. Provided a death notice was put in at the time."

Kebble went over to a recess packed with tall, broad, leather-bound volumes. As he carried one back, clutching it before him so that it entirely concealed his body from neck to knee, Purbright received the grotesque impression of a book walking.

"Last year's," puffed Kebble, setting it with a great slam on the desk.

As if conjured by the sound, Sergeant Worple appeared at that moment in the doorway. "Good morning, Inspector," he called across to Purbright. "They said I'd be likely to find you in here, sir."

"Oh, they did, did they?" Purbright was beginning to wonder if the hidden army of his observers would follow him for the rest of his life, cheerfully and loyally camping at a discreet distance from wherever he might choose to visit.

"Yes, sir," said Warple, unabashed. "Chief Inspector Larch would be much obliged if you could spare him a minute or two as soon as it's convenient."

Purbright said he found it convenient there and then. Before he left he suggested to Kebble that Leaper might enjoy the novelty of seeking the source of the second quotation.

At the police station, Purbright found Larch standing before his desk. He looked rather like a prison governor putting a cheerful, fatherly face on the announcement of a refused stay of execution.

"Come in, Mr Purbright. I have a message for you from the Chief Constable." He pushed back a tray of papers from the front of the desk and perched there, his long fingers drumming his knee. "I don't quite appreciate its significance myself, but doubtless you will understand. He asked me to tell you that the explosive he was worried about has turned up. Or rather" – Larch looked coldly amused – "somebody has discovered that it was never really missing."

"I see," said Purbright.

Larch's smile broadened. "It seems that the Civil Defence Officer had several cases moved to another store two or three months ago so that he could park his golf clubs there. He'd forgotten all about it."

"How very remiss of him."

"Fun and games, eh, Mr Purbright? You didn't tell me you shared the Chief's concern over that explosive. Now I suppose you'll have to – what's the word? – re-orientate your theories."

"Any theories of mine about Biggadyke's death – and I suppose that is what you're talking about – are quite without importance. If you care to think of me as an ineffectual and discredited interloper, by all means do so. Now that this affair has translated itself, as it were, it only remains for me to do likewise." Purbright held out his hand.

"You're not leaving us?"

Purbright smiled pleasantly at the author of this somewhat crude acidity. "Oh, yes," he said, "I'm afraid I must. The traffic's simply dreadful in Flaxborough at this time of year. But I'm sure you'll be able to handle a little local murder case without any help from me."

The expression of sardonic jubilation faded from Larch's face as if he had been knifed from behind. He slipped slowly from the desk, drew himself erect and gave Purbright an agonized stare. "You know that? You're . . . you're sure that's what happened?"

"I'm virtually certain that Biggadyke was murdered. If you want to know why, I'll tell you."

Larch nodded absently. "Yes . . . yes, of course you must tell me." His normally aggressive sibilants were now weak: the whispered evidence of a rather pathetic oral deformity. Purbright described his interview with Leaper. When he had finished, Larch walked round to his chair and sat down. He looked tired, and spoke with obvious effort.

"Mr Purbright: I've a favour to ask of you. It's that you stay on here a little longer."

"That may be difficult. After this week, impossible. Why do you ask?" Purbright had the curious feeling that he was delivering the lines of a bad play.

"Because I don't trust myself to be able to find out the truth of this thing. You see, I am personally involved, though not in the way Hessledine seems to have thought."

Larch's glance fell slightly as he went on: "You won't know this, Mr Purbright, but Biggadyke was what I believe they call a close friend of my wife's. I happen to have learned that they'd arranged to meet that Tuesday night when he was killed. She was to have gone to his caravan. There was nothing to stop her going. I was away from home. And I understand she's pretty punctillious about that sort of appointment." The small twisted smile lasted only an instant. "You see, of course, what I'm afraid of. That Hilda knew what was going to happen. That . . . somehow or other, she'd . . . had a hand in it."

Meeting his eyes, Purbright said quietly: "You know, you're talking absolute nonsense."

"Am I?" Larch brought his fist crashing down on the desk. "Am I, Mr Purbright? Then why in God's name wasn't she there when that thing went off? Why isn't she dead too?"

16

IF THE SIGHT OF PURBRIGHT AND LARCH ENTERING his office together and apparently in amity surprised Mr Kebble he did not show it. But nor did he say anything about the interesting discovery he had just made, which, in the absence of the man he called Old Acid-guts, he would spontaneously have announced.

Purbright, however, went straight to that very point. "The Chief Inspector and I," he said, "are very interested in Celia, Mr Kebble. One might almost say we have high hopes of her."

The editor glanced up at each of the policemen in turn, like a plump poodle flanked by a pair of Afghan hounds. "Celia," he muttered. "Ah, yes . . ."

"Any luck?" Purbright was looking down at the open newspaper file. He caught sight of a column headed in black Gothic type.

Kebble pursed his lips and began moving a stubby, nicotine-stained finger down the page. Larch and Purbright peered at the point where it came at last to a reluctant stop.

They read: 'July 1st, suddenly: Celia Grope, aged 20 years'.

Kebble broke the silence. "That's the only Celia I've been able to find. Mind you, I'm not . . ." His voice tailed off unhappily as he looked up at the graven solemnity of the chief inspector's face.

"We can't let personal feelings worry us now, Mr Kebble," said Larch, sententiously. "You mustn't get the

160

idea that you've let someone down, or anything of that sort." He turned to Purbright. "I suppose you won't have heard about that business?" He nodded towards the year-old newspaper.

"She was knocked down by a car, wasn't she?"

"She was. And you can guess the name of the driver."

"Biggadyke." Purbright saw no reason to point out that he was not guessing.

Larch nodded and stared past him as if looking at a now familiar ghost that he had given up trying to exorcise. "We did our best with a manslaughter charge – that was before the new Act, of course – but it didn't stick. He was very lucky."

"Luckier than Celia."

Larch flicked at him his cold, sad glance. "As you say, Mr Purbright: luckier than Celia."

"And what," Mr Kebble put in, "are you going to do now?" He was beginning to find oppressive the towering proximity of the two men carrying on their conversation over his head.

"Will Grope still be over at the cinema?" Larch asked him.

"He should be."

Kebble watched the policemen go. Larch's purposeful stride took him first to the door. He looked, the editor reflected, like an executioner. Following at a stroll, Purbright turned and smiled. "Thanks for the coffee, Mr Kebble."

The editor smiled weakly and raised his hand. Then his attention was caught by Leaper holding aloft a book and gesticulating. "Oh, Mr Purbright!" he called. The inspector came back to the counter.

"I forgot to tell you," said Kebble, handing him the book, "that Leonard's tracked the other half of that quotation."

"Has he now." Purbright beamed at the youth. "Smart work, Mr Leaper; smart work indeed!" He nearly added

161

'The Commissioner shall hear of this' but refrained on catching an agonized look from Kebble and the murmured warning: "No praise, old chap. Like firewater to an Indian. Queer lad."

The foyer of the cinema was empty. Shafts of sunlight, aswarm with dancing dust motes, slanted from the side windows upon the plastic stucco and struck back a chilly, colour-drained gleam. Where they fell across the carpet, the golden patches were scabbed with innumerable lozenges of blackened, trodden-in chewing gum. There was a smell of ashtrays and vitiated deodorant. Above the whine of a distant vacuum cleaner rose occasionally the cackle of ladies making discoveries under seats.

Larch pulled one of the auditorium doors slightly open and peered through. "Grope's there now," he said to Purbright, "but I'd like to get a few things straight before we have a word with him."

They sat on the outskirts of an enormous chesterfield.

"I suppose," Larch began, "that you're satisfied that whoever sent in that piece of poetry meant it as a hint that Stan Biggadyke had something coming to him?"

Purbright did not answer immediately. He opened the book that Kebble had handed him, found the turned down page, and read a couple of verses to himself.

"Are you familiar," he then asked Larch, "with the works of Emily Dickinson?"

His companion accepted the question as purely rhetorical and began picking his teeth.

"She wrote, among other things," Purbright explained, "a poem piquantly entitled 'There's Been a Death'. The last line of the penultimate verse, together with the whole final verse, read like this:

" 'There'll be that dark parade
Of tassels and of coaches soon;

162

> It's easy as a sign –
> The intuition of the news
> In just a country town' "

Larch disengaged his matchstick. "Tassels and coaches
. . . a funeral, of course."

"Obviously."

"Dark parade . . . I like that bit. Very neatly put." He
frowned. "But you've read out more than there was on the
newspaper cutting. Has that crook Kebble been snipping at
it, do you think?"

"Of course not." Purbright felt a little impatient with
Larch's extravagant view of the criminal propensities of
his fellow citizens. Apart from the likelihood of its being
fatuous and unjust, it kept the field of suspects discon-
certingly packed.

"No, the quotation in the paper ended with 'easy as a
sign' so that there would be a final rhyme with 'divine'.
You remember the first part – 'The thirst that from the soul
doth rise doth ask a drink divine' – the object of that was
twofold. It hinted strongly at vengeance, as Kebble noticed,
and it subtly identified the person whose death was to be
avenged. Ben Jonson's dedication was 'To Celia'. Our
murderer's dedication was to a girl with the same name.
Quite clearly, this Grope female.

"Now, then . . ." – Purbright tapped the open page – "The
lines of Emily Dickinson that have been so oddly welded
to those of Mr Jonson complete the story. It's been most
admirably done, you know. Especially, I think, the
omission of Miss Dickinson's last two lines."

"You said that was just to get a rhyme," Larch pointed
out.

"Primarily, yes. But the force of a quotation is
immensely increased when it is partly submerged, so to
speak. Lawyers, you'll notice, never quote their Latin tags

163

in full. Tempora mutantur, m'lud . . . hrrm, hrrm, careless wave of the hand, judge flattered, case dismissed – you know the sort of thing. But that's very ordinary stuff. Look at what's been left unsaid here . . . 'the intuition of the news in just a country town'. It sums up the whole purpose of this extraordinary notice. Yet the murderer has had the subtlety – and self control – to hide the crux of his message from all but the kind of person who likes to grapple with intellectual literary competitions. He must have an extremely rarefied sense of drama. If this is a symptom of criminal vanity, I'm inclined to think he has something to be vain about."

Larch gazed at a mortician1y tinted portrait of Ramon Navarro on the opposite wall. "It sounds like one of our culture birds to me," he observed. "I told you they were the ones to watch. Hoole was my bet, as I told you, but I suppose Grope's odds-on favourite now."

"Is he cultured?" Purbright asked doubtfully.

Larch snorted. "He's Chalmsbury's poet bloody laureate. What more do you want?"

"I didn't think Mr Grope's poetry was quite in the same category as the stuff we've been talking about. Still, he probably has a fairly catholic taste."

"You know he writes those 'In Memoriams' for the paper, don't you?"

"So I've been told."

"Don't you think, then, that when he set out to do a crafty one for poor old Stan he'd deliberately disguise his style? It strikes me that the simplest way of doing that would have been to pick up a few lines written by one or two other people and mix them up."

"It's conceivable."

Larch shrugged. "Well, then; that's obviously what he did. The rest ties up. He's the father of the girl Stan killed. The accident probably tipped his nut and he's been scheming ever since to take revenge. The anniversary of her death would be just the day."

"The motive's strong enough," Purbright agreed. "What about opportunity?"

"Grope had that, all right. He hangs on here until all sorts of odd times. I've known him sleep all night in one of the seats. He could easily have slipped out to that caravan, got the window open as you suggested, popped the bomb inside and scarpered without anyone being the wiser. His old woman doesn't keep tabs on him."

"And the earlier explosions?"

Larch considered. "Aye, well I suppose he must have worked those too. The same argument applies, though. Grope always had a good excuse for being out at night."

Cradling his shins in clasped hands, Purbright drew up his knees and pensively rested his chin upon them. When again he began to speak, his voice was flattened by the posture and Larch had to bend forward to catch what he said.

"The idea of setting off a chain of explosions in the form of practical jokes for which Biggadyke might be blamed was clever. It had precisely the intended effect. A good many minds were already made up by the time the last explosion was fixed – the only one that really mattered. Even the coroner, who's no fool, was prepared to assume what the murderer intended him to assume. It's important, I think, to grasp that planning of this order indicated an altogether exceptional mind. Unless we do, we might easily fall into whatever second or third line traps that so gifted a gentleman would undoubtedly have devised."

"I would hardly call Grope gifted," said Larch, after pausing to wonder what Purbright was getting at.

"You wouldn't?"

"He's a bit peculiar, but not in the way that would make him a genius. No, this business has just turned out luckily for him, that's all. You're reading too much clever stuff into it."

The stalls door opened and one of the charwomen waddled through. She glanced blankly at the waiting policemen and went into a closet. They could hear her singing a wordless, wavering dirge.

"Will he be long, do you think?" Purbright asked.

Larch rose immediately. "I'll root him out."

"No; don't let's ruffle the fellow. If he's the one you want, it's going to be difficult enough to lead him into court in a friendly way. Pushing him would be hopeless."

Larch smiled sourly, but he sat down again. "Grope's no master mind. I wish you'd get that idea out of your head. I tell you once he sees that we know what's what, he'll give us all we want."

"It's your case."

"I know these people." Larch waved his hand. "They're incapable of elaborate planning and plotting. You said something just now about traps – second and third line traps, wasn't that it?" He waited for Purbright to nod. "Yes, well it's all so much fanny. What did you mean."

Purbright thought that behind the bluster he detected anxiety. He explained quietly.

"It seems to me, d'you know, that whoever removed Mr Biggadyke took good care to build around the killing a number of defences in depth, as it were. Or traps, if you like, in which the inevitable investigation would be caught and either made harmless or turned away against somebody else.

"The first and most intelligently devised trap was very nearly successful in ending the matter. Almost everyone gleefully leaped into it. As I said before, it was the assumption that Biggadyke had killed himself by his own ridiculous prank-playing.

"Certain knowledge was needed for that plan. The

murderer must have been aware firstly of Biggadyke's reputation as a practical joker – no difficulty there, of course. Secondly, he must have had a good idea of the sort of targets Biggadyke would choose. You'll admit the selection was most convincing. The third piece of knowledge could have been acquired only by careful observation – or else" – Purbright regarded Larch steadily – "by receiving or overhearing a confidence. I'm talking now of Biggadyke's private arrangements for Tuesday nights, his caravan appointments.

"So much for the preparation of trap number one. All very ingenious and thorough. But there was one danger...." He paused.

"Your wife, Mr Larch."

The Chief Inspector said nothing. He slowly brought up his hand and looked at the open palm as if examining a derisory tip.

"The odds were that she would keep clear, as indeed she has," Purbright went on. "But there was always the possibility of her telling the truth about those Tuesday nights. Once that was out, the misadventure set-up would collapse. And the fact of murder would be left in broad view.

"As it happens, we spotted it from a completely different direction. But that was by the sheer luck of Kebble's having seized on that queer obituary.

"The murderer was intelligent enough to realize that by the very act of intervening and thereby destroying his first defence Mrs Larch would prove the perfect decoy into trap number two. Once she allowed her relationship with Biggadyke to be known, suspicion would automatically fall on the man with the best reason in the world for wishing her lover dead – the man who, by curious coincidence, is another of the town's regular Tuesday night absentees – and, to crown it all, the man who is an expert in the use of explosives, a quantity of which happens to have been missed from the depot where he is a part-time instructor."

Larch drew in a long, rustling breath. The grey face had whitened round the mouth. Yet he forced his thin, humourless smile. "We'd better get the bastard pulled in before you make me confess."

"Mrs Weaver!"

Both men looked to see the face of Mr Grope thrust through the auditorium door. Again rose the querulous bleat: "Mrs We-e-e-eaver!"

There was a clatter of buckets and dustpans and the charwoman emerged from her haven, blinking and hostile.

"Kindly bring a paper bag, Mrs Weaver. Third one-and-nine from the radiator on the clock side. Seventh seat in."

The woman glowered. "That Mr Follicle's not been taking 'is bandage off again?"

"Looks like it, Mrs Weaver."

Grope spotted Purbright and Larch as they rose. He shook his head. "You mustn't start the queue inside, sir," he said reprovingly, adding after further scrutiny, "You are patrons, I suppose?"

"No, Mr Grope, we are not," retorted Larch. "I think you know who I am. Would you mind coming over here a minute?"

Grope lumbered up, looking from one to the other. Mrs Weaver, incurious, padded purposefully away. "Now then," Larch said, "you'll kindly do your duty by answering a few questions. You've nothing to be nervous about if you tell the truth."

"What kind of questions?" asked Grope sullenly.

"All kinds." Larch was plunging into the interview with a horrid briskness that prompted Purbright to nudge his arm and frown. Larch misinterpreted this as a request to be introduced. "Oh, yes; this is a colleague of mine. Inspector Purbright. And if you think my questions are rough, just you wait until he starts."

Grope gazed mournfully at Purbright and began button-ing up his long, green commissionaire's coat. He looked like a bewildered old general, captured in a washroom miles behind the lines.

"How long," Larch was asking, "have you been working here?"

"Fourteen years, or very near." The rhyme flowed out so effortlessly that Larch did not notice it; he merely felt Grope's reply to be indefinably insolent.

"And who employed you up to then?"

"I was at Barlow's foundry . . . gentlemen."

Larch scowled. He still could not place what it was about this docile, cheese-faced fellow that annoyed him. "What sort of work were you doing there?"

"Tool-room fitting . . . it took some care."

"Precision engineering, eh?"

Grope, perplexed by the sudden appearance of a predatory gleam in Larch's eye, hesitated and then blurted out: "That's all I am going to say today."

Larch looked at him with contemptuous disbelief. "Surely you realise the inadvisability of an obstructive attitude. My colleague and I are investigating a serious matter."

Grope sat down on the chesterfield. He looked prepared to withstand a seige.

Larch spoke softly in Purbright's ear. "He's fly, this one. You followed the point about engineering? Those bombs. Could be." To Grope he said: "Now let's be sensible, shall we? Can you remember what you were doing on Tuesday, July the first?"

"No."

"Come along. You haven't even thought about it. It was the night Mr Biggadyke was killed. Remember?"

Grope probed his ear with his little finger.

"You were seen out in the town that night," Larch persisted. "Quite late. How about telling us where you went?"

"Home."

"Before that. Stop being awkward."

"Go away," Grope said.

Larch looked at Purbright with mock surprise. "He'd like us to go away. I wonder why?" Purbright's eyes closed in despair as Larch turned back on his victim and rasped: "You had a pretty strong grudge against Biggadyke, didn't you?"

The commissionaire remained silent.

"You hadn't forgotten what happened to your daughter, had you? That was on July the first. Just a year ago, wasn't it?"

Purbright tried desperately to think of some way to block this preposterous inquisition. He saw on Grope's otherwise expressionless face a twitch of annoyance, or of pain.

"You don't have to be ashamed of your feelings, Grope," Larch went on. "You were bound to feel cut up. Even a bit vengeful, perhaps. Is that it? Understandable, you know. Your own flesh and blood."

This embarrassing parody of Hollywood third-degree, Purbright knew, was simply Larch's way of taking reprisal for the destruction of his own self-confidence. He was like a blinded man still lashing out when his torturers had departed. But he would have to be restrained somehow. Purbright coughed and was about to interpose a firm "It seems to me . . ." when he was put off his stroke by a totally unexpected reply from Grope.

"Flesh and blood?" he echoed. "Flesh and blood nothing. If you're talking about poor Celia, you've got it all mixed up."

Larch looked up at the ceiling. "Ah. Mixed up. Thank you, Grope." He glared down again. "I suppose you're going to tell me she wasn't your daughter."

"No, I'm not. But you were talking about flesh and blood.

And Celia wasn't. Not ours, I mean. We adopted her."

Purbright seized his chance. "Now, Mr Grope . . ." – he sat beside him – "there seems to have been some little misunderstanding. This news of yours is interesting."

"Why?" Grope countered, with no sign of finding his new interrogator any less provocative. "We never pretended the baby was ours."

"No, but twenty years is a long time. Things can come to be taken for granted. Tell me, Mr Grope; did you know who Celia's real parents were – her natural parents?"

Grope said nothing.

"You don't know?"

"Things like that are confidential."

Seeing Larch prepared to swoop in once more, Purbright gently waved discouragement. To Grope he said: "They are indeed. You are fully entitled to keep Celia's origin secret if you wish. On the other hand, you could save us a certain amount of time – in record searching and all that, you know – by telling us now."

It was a poor inducement, as Purbright knew. But Grope was of an essentially helpful disposition. In any case, the ponderous process of deduction which had been going on in his head ever since Larch opened his assault had now produced something the effect of which he was anxious to enjoy there and then.

He looked away from Purbright and stared boldly at Larch.

"Celia was put out for adoption by Mr and Mrs Pointer," he announced. "That was straight after she was born, of course. But even so you might say she was really your sister-in-law, Mr Larch. Mightn't you?"

17

AMELIA POINTER RECEIVED PURBRIGHT IN THE
garden. Although the shock of acquiring one as a son-in-
law had almost worn off, she still regarded policemen with
considerable apprehension. Like open umbrellas, they were
unlucky things to have in the house.

Hilda had answered the door, prepared her mother for
the requested interview ("He looks quite human actually")
and made introductions. She now stood protectively beside
Mrs Pointer and motioned Purbright to have his say.

"This isn't going to be terribly easy," he began.

"No, of course not," said Hilda, looking very much at
ease. Mrs Pointer shook her head and gave a little smile.

"You may have heard from Mr Larch," Purbright went
on, "that further inquiries are being made into the death
of Mr. Biggadyke."

Hilda spotted some seed pods on a spike of lupins and
began nipping them off. "No," she said.

"Oh. I thought he might have mentioned it. Never mind.
The point is, you might be able to help us, Mrs Pointer –
in an indirect way."

"Mother will be pleased to do what she can." Hilda
stretched in search of further seed pods. Her movements
were lithe and confident.

"We have a notion, you see – there may be absolutely
nothing in it, of course, but you know how policemen move
round and round a thing – we have this notion that some
connection could exist between a girl called Celia Grope
and the way Mr Biggadyke . . . passed on."

Mrs Pointer's lips fluttered like comatose moths suddenly stimulated by a touch.

"Do you know anyone called Celia Grope, mother?" Hilda asked her cheerfully. "No, Inspector; it seems that she doesn't."

"But you did, didn't you, Mrs Larch?"

She eyed him shrewdly. "I vaguely remember the name. Wasn't she the girl who was killed in a street accident some time last year? Or passed on from one, perhaps you'd say?"

Purbright ungrudgingly marked Hilda one up.

"Neither of you ladies knew Miss Grope?"

"Not personally, no."

"Mrs Pointer?" Purbright did not enjoy being rude but he felt that Hilda Larch was more likely to respect tactics than tact. However, the snub to the older woman's guardian and interpreter was of no avail; Mrs Pointer merely looked helplessly at her daughter.

"Celia Grope was an adopted child. Her father told us that much and it was a fairly simple matter to trace her natural parentage from the court records. I tell you this," Purbright explained, "in case you imagine I have come here to fish for information. I haven't. The facts have been landed, so to speak. All I ask is a little assistance in weighing them up."

"You are a very devious policeman," said Hilda, "and a mysterious one. Won't you say what this business is all about and what it has to do with us?"

Purbright sighed. "Obviously that is what I must do. I had hoped that making painful revelations was not going to be required. You, Mrs Pointer, know perfectly well what I am talking about. If your daughter really doesn't know, don't you think it would be kinder if you told her now yourself?"

Before Hilda could provide an answer on her mother's behalf, Mrs Pointer broke her silence.

"Twenty years!"

The inspector was startled by the vehemence packed into the two words by a woman who had seemed to possess no more independent motivation than a ventriloquist's doll. The cry was a harsh compound of anger, pain and pleading.

Hilda stared at her mother. From her slowly unclenching hand lupin pods, bruised and split, dropped to the grass.

"Did you have to?" Mrs Pointer made as if to clutch Purbright's sleeve but her arm remained faltering in mid-air like the limb of a crippled beggar.

A bee droned erratically round their heads. Hilda started, as if from sleep. She pulled out a case and matches from the pockets of her slacks, lit a cigarette, and released a tremulous "Oh, for God's sake!" with the first drag of smoke.

Mrs Pointer regarded her appealingly. "There seemed no point in telling you dear. Celia never knew." She looked down at her own hands, pulling at the stuff of her skirt. "I tried to think of her as having been born dead. But of course I couldn't. It was. . . ." The lips went on moving for a few seconds longer but no words came. Purbright was reminded of an old film running on when the sound track had failed.

Hilda had had time to throw a cloak of anger over her bewilderment and wretchedness. "I take it," she said coldly, "that you and Daddy had some compelling reason for this extraordinary arrangement?"

"Your father thought . . . he said it would be better. . . ."

Hilda turned abruptly to Purbright. "I'm sorry if you find this embarrassing. Sordid disclosures always read rather better than they sound. You did ask for it, though."

The policeman shook his head. He spoke gently. "Embarrassment is a selfish emotion, Mrs Larch. I think we can be of much greater help to one another at the moment if we dispense with it."

"Oh, let's be clinical, then. You take over the questioning and we'll have a post-mortem on my sister." She flashed a look at her mother. "Or half-sister, should I say?"

Purbright watched Mrs Pointer but she showed no reaction. "Is that true, Mrs Pointer?" he asked her. Was the adoption arranged because your husband knew he was not the child's father?"

The woman tightened her mouth and seemed to be marshalling strength for another attempt at the unaccustomed exercise of speech.

"He had been to France, hadn't he?" Purbright prompted. "Was that something to do with it?"

Mrs Pointer moved closer to Hilda and accepted the arm that she slipped, almost absent-mindedly, round her shoulder. "I'm sorry," the mother said. They were the only words she had been able to summon. Her life, thought Purbright, must have become a single, dreary act of apology. He felt sadness, yet no compassion.

"Have you anything more to ask, Inspector?" Hilda had resumed her role of manager.

"Yes," said Purbright, deliberately. "I should like to be told the name of Celia's father."

"I . . . I can't tell you that."

"Please believe me: this is not idle and impertinent curiosity. The matter is important and perhaps urgent."

Mrs Pointer shook her head. The action was more like a shudder.

"He's still alive?"

"Yes," she whispered. "Oh. yes."

"And living here in the town?"

She made no reply.

"Tell me, Mrs Pointer: had this man maintained a relationship with Celia over the years? Not necessarily as a father, I mean, but an affectionate relationship."

"He used to see her, I believe."

"They were fond of each other?"

"Oh, yes." The words emerged dreamily, enviously.

"Won't you tell me his name?"

The ghost of an old pride stirred in the faded frightened little woman. She looked directly into Purbright's face. "Certainly not," she said.

Purbright and Hilda left her there in the garden. She was kneeling beside some border plants, fussily easing them apart.

At the front door, Hilda Larch hesitated. "Why couldn't they have told me? Now there's so much . . . so much I can't put right in my mind."

Purbright said nothing. She passed a hand across her brow. "It's too late."

After a while she looked up at him. "That man who killed Celia. . . ."

"Biggadyke."

"Yes. He . . . I let him make love to me." The muscles of her neck were tightly drawn.

"I see."

She stroked the knob of the Yale lock with her palm "You think, don't you . . . that Celia's father . . ."

"Murdered. . . ."

Her eyes blazed. "Executed, you mean!"

"That probably is a better word."

She nodded. "I'm glad mother said no more. Goodbye, Inspector."

On the step he turned. "There's just one thing, Mrs Larch."

She waited.

"That night when Biggadyke was killed – why did you decide to stay away from his caravan?"

A slow, careful smile passed over her face. "I had a telephone message, Inspector. From the Civil Defence people. They said my husband had finished early and was on his way home."

"And was he?"

"There must have been some mistake. He arrived the following day – as usual."

"The voice on the telephone. . . ."

Her smile broadened. "Absolutely unidentifiable, Inspector, I assure you. But I liked it. I liked it tremendously."

The door closed.

Purbright walked slowly down the path. He was searching his memory for something he knew had matched an impression just received. It was as though he had emerged from a market knowing that on two separate stalls were pictures or ornaments which, though unremarkable each in itself, once had formed a pair. He recalled Mrs Pointer's pale, bewildered face; its expression of constant readiness to register regret for something. Had he seen it before? He thought not. Years of self-immolation had left it almost devoid of memorable peculiarities.

Hilda's, then? Handsome, bitter, faintly mocking. He pictured Hilda Larch hiding intense shock and disgust beneath the simple mechanics of lighting a cigarette; she had managed it with the brusque carelessness of a horse-woman between gymkhana events. The sense of an un-placed resemblance grew stronger. It was something to do with Hilda, perhaps her whole features and bearing, or at least some look or mannerism of hers, that Purbright had seen in another person since his arrival in Chalmsbury.

He tried to conjure a mental identification parade, but it was no use. The faces blurred and merged, like images in wind-ruffled water. He crossed to the shaded side of the road and sauntered, with blank mind and painfully hot feet, back into the town.

Larch, in shirt sleeves, sat at his desk by an open window. He looked cool, but unrelaxed. Purbright gave him a somewhat dessicated account of his afternoon's visiting.

"What a good job you're a policeman, Mr Purbright. The husbands of bitches are terribly prone to be blackmailed. Did you know that?"

The pleasantry was ignored. Larch tried another. "Well, have you found poor Stanley's bloody murderer?"

"Certainly."

"Go on, then, Mr Purbright."

"He's your mother-in-law's lover."

Larch stared, his face twisted as if he were trying to catch a scarcely audible sound. Then, suddenly, his jaw dropped like an excavator bucket and there emerged a guffaw that turned Sergeant Worple, sitting in the charge room fifty feet away, pale with alarm.

When the short spasm was over, Purbright demurely corrected himself. "Former lover, I should have said, of course."

"Yes, by God you should!" A rumbling echo of amusement sounded in Larch's gullet. "But it doesn't take you much further does it? I'm afraid our filing system doesn't run to records of the ex-boy friends of the town's middle-aged ladies."

"We might not need records. There are pretty long and retentive memories in a place like this."

"Retentive in more than one sense. They don't open up in the name of the law, believe me."

Purbright looked at Larch thoughtfully. "Excuse my asking, but you're a few years older than your wife, aren't you?"

"What the hell's that to do with it?"

"Only that it struck me that you might remember something yourself of what went on here twenty years ago. Gossip, you know. Were you around then?"

"I was, as it happens. But I hadn't married into the bloody Pointers."

"I didn't mean family gossip – just parade room talk."

Larch leaned back with a sigh. "Look, son: this was a real police force in the 'thirties. We didn't sit around over tea and knitting. If you think . . ."

"Mr Larch," Purbright interrupted firmly, "I don't much mind your being aggressive, obtuse, bombastic and generally offensive. What I shall not tolerate, though, is the old copper gaff. Now, do we understand each other?"

There was a long silence. Then Larch gave a slight, dismissive wave of the hand and looked down as though calculating something rather difficult.

"No," he said quietly at last, "I can't recall a damn thing that might give you a lead. I knew the Pointers, of course. Not intimately; I hadn't met Hilda then. And I remember something about Ozzy going over to France. That's all."

"How old would his wife have been?"

"Thirty, thirty-fivish."

"Promiscuous?"

Larch seemed almost shocked. "Damn it, man. You've seen her. Even twenty years. . . ."

"Perhaps not," Purbright agreed. "We'll give her credit for having been selective. It was probably a genuine first-and-last romance. And as discreet as a spinster buying a bottle of scent." He paused. "Yet there was something. . . .

"Tell me," said Purbright, suddenly brisk, "you knew this Celia girl, I suppose?"

"Only by sight."

"That's what I mean. Would you say she showed resemblance to anyone in particular?"

"I realize now that she was remarkably like my wife."

Purbright nodded. "That's understandable. Anyone else? Anyone exceptionally tall, for instance?"

"Tall?"

"Whoever stuck those bombs on the statue and that shop

sign thing must have had a phenomenal reach. And no short man could have climbed the park railings, either; remember that the water fountain could only have been mined after the park closed."

"What about a ladder? A box, even?"

"Too noticeable. It might have served for the park business, but not for the jobs in the main streets on clear summer nights. They were done very neatly. A quick approach, a quick departure, no messing about."

Larch picked up his pen and peered into one of his trays. "Sounds a principle worth copying," he remarked. "Anyway, I thought you were going to use this . . . this holiday of yours to get some sunshine."

Purbright rose slowly from his chair, walked to the window and stood gazing absently at the roofs of the buildings beyond the courtyard.

"Sunshine," he repeated. "Of course. No, I don't want to miss that."

As the inspector strolled across the Borough Bridge, glancing down over the massive, shabby cast-iron parapet into the ebbing river, he tried to decide what he should do about the killer of the unmourned Mr Biggadyke.

He recognized, and half-admired, the parochial loyalties, compounded with a sort of pagan amorality, that made the people of Chalmsbury policeman-proof. Although he normally enjoyed his job, if only as an exercise in ingenuity, he had no illusion of being an instrument of absolute justice. Some kinds of crime made him angry; none made him righteous. He gave every criminal credit for knowing, if not what he had been about, at least what he didn't want to have happen to him in consequence. In this he was different from most policemen, who take as a personal insult the unwillingness of a wrongdoer to be caught.

Purbright was also well aware that the public is less

zealous to see the triumph of the law than it likes to pretend. Its diffidence was shown in Chalmsbury to a degree suggestive of a Robin Hood fixation. Could long years of rule by men like Larch have been responsible, he wondered.

None would blame him – perhaps he would not blame himself – for slipping out of this town that was so obviously content to allow the false interpretation of Biggadyke's death to stand as the official record. He had some sympathy with this communal conspiracy to let a dead dog lie.

By the time he reached Mrs Crispin's front door and let himself into the cool, dark lobby, smelling of mackintoshes and vinegar, Purbright was very nearly resigned to desertion.

He went into the dining room. The table was set already for two, but his fellow lodger had not yet arrived. Purbright picked up the copy of the *Chalmsbury Chronicle* which had been put by Payne's plate and sat down to await his meal.

The report of the inquest, solidly set and so explicitly headlined in depth as to render the reading of the matter beneath almost superfluous, had been given pride of place on one of the centre pages. Purbright began to scan it rapidly and without much interest.

Then, as he turned into the second column, his eye did what a car will do on being taken round a sharp bend too quickly and inattentively. It skidded and came to rest in column three.

The inspector went on staring at the photograph before him while the truth about Biggadyke's murder took sharp and clear form like a crystal growing out of a suddenly cooled concentrate.

After perhaps half a minute he looked down and read the caption.

"Mr Joseph Mulvaney, senior projectionist at the Rialto Cinema, Chalmsbury, has been nominated to receive the Grand Brooch of Erin, an honour conferred upon Irish nationals ordinarily resident in this country for outstanding service in the cause of Anglo-Irish relations. Mr Mulvaney (pictured here in the projection room where he has worked for the past twelve years) hopes to be able to travel to Dublin to receive his award in person when the presentations are made next Tuesday."

18

PURBRIGHT FOLDED THE PAPER AND REPLACED IT
on the table. He went in search of Mrs Crispin. The only
occupant of the kitchen was Phyllis, shaping fishcakes with
the nonchalant expertise of a prize-fighter's masseur. She
bathed him in her dimpled sir-she-said smile and said that
the Missus had gone out for the evening but that his tea
was on the way.

"Has Mr Payne not come in yet?"

She slid the first of the fish cakes into the frying pan.
"Not unless he went straight up to his room. I suppose his
car will be at the door if he's here."

"No, it isn't." Purbright cast a nervous glance at the blue
cloud rising from the pan and returned to the lobby. He
opened the front door and looked out, then walked
quickly and quietly up the stairs.

There was no answer to his knock on Payne's door. He
pushed it open. The room was as he had last seen it; tidy,
ordinary, and wearing the faintly depressing air common to
all apartments, whether prison cells or bed-sitters, in which
a man must share his dreams with his shoe brushes.

Purbright took a step towards the bookcase and stopped.
In the photograph frame on its top shelf there was only the
white card backing. The picture of the little girl standing
by what he had mistakenly assumed to be a television
camera had been removed.

Not that it mattered greatly now. He was clearly aware
that it was the child's face he had seen in the features of
Hilda Larch. Solemnly staring out upon Cornelius Payne's

lonely little world had been Celia, photographed ten or twelve years ago – probably by her foster father – in the projection room of the cinema where he worked.

He knelt and began looking through the titles of Payne's books. Palgrave's 'Golden Treasury' was among them, and next to it an anthology of modern verse. He took out the anthology and opened it by its ribbon marker. Half way down the left-hand page was the poem by Emily Dickinson. "There's been a death . . ." it began. Purbright closed the book and put it back.

In the textbook on organic chemistry he found the chapter dealing with nitro-compounds to which Payne had made his deceptively cool and co-operative reference. The instructions for making nitro-glycerin were full and precise. Purbright thought it sounded an eminently feasible operation, given laboratory equipment and expert caution. The fragment of a conversation drifted into his mind. Kebble had spoken in the same breath of Payne and the Nobel Prize. Nobel . . . inventor of dynamite : the man who discovered that the dangerously unstable nitrate of glycerin could be tamed by soaking it into a subsance called kieselguhr.

Purbright searched further along the shelf. At the end, among three or four volumes in faded but undamaged bindings that suggested they were old school prizes, was one entitled 'A Boy's Dictionary of Natural Substances'. Without much hope, he thumbed through to the K's. It was there. Kieselguhr.

'Kieselguhr, or Infusorial Earth, by which name it is known in the jewellery trade, is a fine powder used as a polishing agent. It is also an ingredient of dynamite.'

Downstairs a door slammed. Purbright hurriedly replaced the book and left the room, closing the door. From the landing he heard Phyllis stun the dining-room table with a plate of fishcakes. Immediately after came his summons to tea. It was like a prairie cattle call. The inspector descended and told her that he would eat as soon as he had made a short telephone call from the lobby. Payne, he noticed, still had not returned.

Larch received Purbright's revelation with a grunt and, "What did I tell you?"

"You didn't tell me anything," Purbright justifiably observed.

"Never mind. Go on."

"It might be as well if I waited here for him. He's late, but that's not to say he won't come. Meanwhile you might like to see if he's still at his shop. A search warrant wouldn't come amiss, incidentally."

"Why?"

"There could be stuff there that you'll need in evidence. Chemicals, lab equipment and so on. It will probably be a job for a Home Office fellow, but at least you can get the place locked up. Invoices might be interesting, too; check deliveries of something called Infusorial Earth. And don't let your blokes fiddle with powders – Payne probably used some kind of home-made fulminate to set his things off."

"Listen: I'm not a bloody Harwell professor."

"That's all right. Leave it to Worple: there's nothing he doesn't know. I'll be here if you want me but as far as I can see it's all yours now." Purbright tried not to sound too relieved.

Larch said everything would be attended to, but he only hoped he was not being let in for an almighty balls-up.

Purbright said he hoped so, too.

"By the way," he added, "do you happen to remember where it was that Biggadyke ran down the Grope girl?"

"Of course. It was in Watergate Street. Quite near Payne's shop, as a matter of fact. Payne never came forward to say she'd been there. It was hardly relevant at the time, though, was it?"

"Not at the time, no." Purbright rang off.

Within the next few hours Purbright answered the telephone four times.

The first two calls were from Larch, anxious to know if Payne had returned. The shop, he said, had been found in the charge of a young man with the intelligence quotient of a sea anemone. Not only was he ignorant of his employer's whereabouts; he seemed uncertain of whether he had ever met him. At least he had not been obstructive. The shop was now locked and guarded. A proper search had not yet been made but at first sight it did look as if some of Purbright's guesses might prove correct.

Purbright gravely acknowledged the tribute and asked whether Larch contemplated putting out a general call for Payne to be held for questioning. Larch retorted that this, of course had been done. He then rang off in order to do it.

The third call was from Sergeant Worple, who explained that he was just checking on the chief inspector's behalf. Purbright informed him, a little tartly, that Payne was still missing – as Mr Larch might well have adduced from the fact that he, Purbright, had not telephoned to the contrary.

"I quite understand that, sir," said Worple, unruffled. "Logic's a great help, even in these days." He paused to let Purbright make what he could of this obliquity and went on : "I thought you might be interested to know that wherever Mr Payne is he hasn't taken his car. It was outside his shop."

"Really?"

"Yes sir. You possibly have never noticed it yourself, but it's quite an old-fashioned model with what they call a sunshine roof. A sliding panel in the top. I mention that because it explains something that has probably been puzzling you."

Purbright relieved his feelings by glaring cross-eyed

at the telephone mouthpiece and sticking out his tongue.

The unhurried, provocatively respectful voice droned on.

"You see, sir, it's quite clear now that Mr Payne was able to fix his explosive devices on the statue and the shop sign by taking his car right up to the target, as you might call it, and standing up on the driving seat through the sunshine roof. It wouldn't take him a minute; then he could sit down again and drive off. All unbeknown," Worple added extravagantly.

"He could have used the same method to get over the park railings, couldn't he, Sergeant?"

"Undoubtedly, sir."

"Did the Chief Inspector work all that out?"

There was a brief silence. "He gave me that impression, sir." Worple sounded like a man counting short change.

"Well, well. It does him credit. I'll give you a call if there are any further developments at this end."

It was some time after ten o'clock when the telephone rang for the fourth time.

"Purbright speaking."

He heard a resonant click as the button in a public call box was pressed.

"It's Payne here."

Purbright swallowed. This he had not expected.

"Oh, yes, Mr Payne?" Did one deliver a formal caution when a man whose arrest one had been trying to contrive suddenly popped up on the telephone?

"Look," the faint, strained voice was saying, "I rather feel I owe you something?"

"Yes?" I must sound like a deaf charlady offering to take a message, Purbright thought.

"I was going to leave you a note, but the idea seemed far from satisfactory. Awfully impersonal, and I'd probably have left out just the things you wanted to know. . . ."

"Where are you speaking from, Mr Payne?"

"Where? Oh, I don't think that matters, does it? You can hear me all right, I suppose."

"Yes, I can hear you. . . ." Purbright looked up to see Mrs Crispin, hatted and mildly Guinness-glad, closing the front door behind her. He beckoned and began writing quickly on the pad by the phone. She came and stood amiably at his side, like a lama waiting for a sugar lump.

"You know what happened, of course," Payne was saying. "Those questions of yours last night were far too inspired to be passed off as what I believe policemen call routine inquiries. It was decent of you to give me a start like that, but I don't want to get away. I don't think I ever did, really. All that elaboration . . . oh, I can't think why I bothered."

"It was rather well done," Purbright said quietly. He pulled the sheet from the pad with his free hand and gave it to Mrs Crispin. Her grin faded as she read the message. Then she glided with surprising speed off to the kitchen and squawked for Phyllis.

"The notice in the paper was silly, wasn't it," Payne said. He sounded tired and the words had a flat clumsiness like those of a man whose tongue is thickened with thirst. "I'm rather ashamed of it now. Pure exhibitionism. Criminals are supposed to find that sort of thing irresistable. Does justice become a crime when it's put on a do-it-yourself basis? I don't know. . . ."

Purbright could hear fast, interrupted breathing, as if Payne was opening and closing his mouth, trying to find the right way to say something. Then, almost conversationally, Payne spoke again. "You know about Celia, I expect?"

"A certain amount. I've guessed, too. There was that photograph in your room."

"It's the only one I have. Old Grope took it a long time

188

ago and let me have a print. He's always been very decent to both of us. He used to send the kid along to the shop on some specious errand or other so that I could keep seeing her."

Purbright glanced at his watch. "Tell me, Mr Payne. . . ."

In the house next door Phyllis had replaced a phone and was trying to explain to its anxious owner the reasons (which she did not understand herself) for the 999 call she had just made.

At Fen Street Chief Inspector Larch was demanding from a night operator at Chalmsbury exchange the location of the kiosk connected with Chalmsbury 4116.

Within that kiosk, which Larch was about to be told was a few yards from the entrance to the municipal cemetery, a tall man clutching a parcel under his left arm bowed his head wearily as he listened to the question that was being put to him.

"How did I know?" he repeated. "By much the same process as Kebble's young reporter adopted, I suppose. It wasn't too difficult to establish Biggadyke's habits. They were" – he smiled faintly in the dusk – "remarkably regular in their way."

Again he listened. The man at the other end of the wire was asking something else and taking his time in doing so. Two minutes went by. Payne leaned against the side of the kiosk. Now and again he glanced at the parcel he held.

"You're quite right," he said. "Hilda told you about that call, did she? It seemed the most effective means of keeping her away that night. I only hope. . . ."

He broke off and stared through the glass. The headlamp beams of an approaching car swept the roadside colonnade of trees fifty yards away, swung round and bore upon the kiosk. He heard the plunging tone of the engine as the driver braked.

Payne slammed the receiver clumsily on its rest, heaved

open the door and ran for the cemetery drive. Larch and a uniformed constable raced after him.

The pursuit was short. After two turns along paths that he seemed to know well, Payne leaped a low box border hedge, took a few staggering steps across turf in which buttercups glimmered, and sank down upon a year-old grave. He clutched the parcel high up against his chest. . . .

Purbright was still holding the dead phone when the sound of the explosion reached him.

More modern fiction from Methuen